BODO

THE TALE OF THE WOODCARVER'S DOG

BY M. D. ADAMS
AND L. E. ADAMS

Published by BookSurge Publishers
5341 Dorchester Road, Suite 16
North Charleston, SC 29418

This book is fiction and all names, places, characters, and events are fictitious. Any resemblance to actual persons, either living or dead, is purely coincidental and not intended by the authors.

To order additional copies please contact BookSurge, LLC
www.booksurge.com or orders@booksurge.com
Copyright © 2006 Mike Adams and Louise Adams

ISBN # 1-4196-2453-9
Library of Congress Control Number: 2006901763

Cover design and book layout by
Studio West of Toughkenamon, PA
studiow@pond.com

Dedication

To every soul who has ever been loved by a dog.
Also to AJ, Lindsay, Pearlie, Jessie, Angel,
Gelica and Max
and to the memory of
Poppy, Zack, Nip, Gin-Gin and Nellie.

❖ ❖ ❖

Acknowledgments

We wish to thank the following people for
their contribution to the story of Bodo.

Mike Adams Jr.
for the writing of the prologue.

Eric Adams and Mike Adams Jr.
for their contributions to the story.

Birgit Clarke
for her knowledge of the German language.

Table of Contents

VI

The German people refer to May 8th, 1945 as *"Stunde Null."*
It means "Zero Hour": the day that life began again.

In the decades that followed World War II, these
determined people would strive with diligence and
fortitude to rebuild their shattered lives, families and
national heritage, and to reclaim their place in the world.
In so doing, through their driving pursuit of perfection in
all aspects of life, they would bring to that world many
wonderful gifts.

This is a story about one of those gifts.

BODO

THE TALE OF THE WOODCARVER'S DOG

"You must rest now, my liebchen.

You have done well. Two beautiful puppies!

Especially this big fellow——

So much the image of his famous grandsire.

Maybe one day he too will be a champion.

I think I will call him Bodo."

PROLOGUE

The dog's sudden bark startled Stefan, causing his hammer to miss and smash his own thumb. *"This is your fault,"* he yelled, as he held up his throbbing thumb toward the big dog, not that the dog cared or even understood.

Stefan turned back to his work and muttered as he drove the last nail, without missing this time, into the last board over the windows. Boarding up houses of lost loved ones, especially those he knew and cared about, gave him little satisfaction. Because Triberg was such a tiny village, tucked away deep in Germany's Black Forest, it was impossible *not* to know everyone, making it especially difficult to do this unpleasant part of his job.

As Triberg's only field agent, he was the one called out to deal with estates when no family members were left.

Stefan had gotten the call yesterday afternoon to secure the cabin and collect the old man's possessions. He had found, or rather heard, the dog as he pulled up.

The frantic howling was coming from the tiny shed behind the cabin. He approached cautiously and eased open the door. Inside he found a large wooden crate with the source of the commotion locked inside it. He had forgotten old man Bremik always had a dog at his side. He was suddenly heart-sick that he had put off the trip until morning, causing the dog to suffer through the freezing night without food, water, or its master.

He had immediately opened the crate door and let the suffering dog out, noticing to his astonishment that the crate was clean and dry. *Poor thing.* He shook his head as he watched the dog disappear into the forest. "Sorry about that, boy!" he yelled after him.

As Stefan loaded up the meager earthly possessions the old hermit had left behind, the dog returned. He hung close to Stefan's side, whimpering softly, it's breath visible in the chilly air. Stefan paid the dog no heed as he struggled to hoist the heavy crate onto the truck. He could not help but notice how beautifully crafted it was, made of solid fir planks tightly pegged and joined with precise hand-cut joints. Well, after all, he thought, Herr Ivo Bremik was a craftsman. Ivo was, in fact, a master woodcarver of the intricate wooden cuckoo clocks for which this region of Germany was famous.

With the dog loaded up and the cabin now secure,

Stefan made one final round about the property, crunching through the deep snow with every step.

CHAPTER ONE
THE PHONE CALL

Traveling the steep and winding snow-covered roads of Baden-Württemberg, Germany, in March was no easy task, and the trip back would be slow. With plenty of time to think, as he carefully negotiated the treacherous twists and turns of the icy mountain road, Stefan found his thoughts drifting back to the first time he had met Herr Ivo Bremik.

It was the spring of his ninth year. In those days the old couple lived on the edge of the village of Triberg in a little Tudor-style cottage. The Bremiks had moved there that same year after selling their large farm outside of Hannover. Ivo was born in Triberg sixty-four years earlier and had always dreamed of someday returning to the quaint and beautiful village of his childhood. They had chosen the little cottage because of its wonderful old-fashioned walled-in garden. At the back of the garden stood an old wooden gate, which opened onto a meadow. At the edge of the meadow, rose the tall silhouettes of the dense fir trees that marked the edge of the ancient and majestic Black Forest.

Stefan had been wandering along the edge of the forest gathering wild mushrooms, something he had been doing with his mother for as long as he could remember. That day he had set out on his own for the first time. He knew exactly where to look. He beamed with pride as he filled his little leather knapsack to the top. As he was about to make his way home, he froze in his tracks at the distant sound of a pack of wild dogs crashing and howling through the underbrush toward him.

Terrified, he scrambled as fast as he could up the nearest tree, spilling his knapsack. He quickly reached the highest branch, his heart pounding, his head filled with stories he had heard about wild dogs devouring their kill limb by limb. He clung as tightly as he could as the sound of the pack got increasingly louder. Suddenly, two large dogs were upon him. Yelping and barking, they leapt high in the air toward him.

He screamed in terror. Then, above the commotion of the dogs, he heard a loud whistle. At once the dogs fell silent and vanished back into the brush toward the sound. The man made his way toward the tree while looking up to where the boy still clung tightly. He gave another command and the dogs instantly re-appeared.

They dropped flat to the ground at their master's feet. Stefan smiled at the memory of Herr Bremik lifting him, still trembling and sobbing, down from his perch and introducing him to his two extremely friendly and rambunctious boxers.

That was when Ivo's wife Beata was still alive. After her death Ivo had left the sunny cottage by the meadow and secluded himself in the tiny wooden cabin deep in the heart of the Black Forest.

As far as Stefan knew, old man Bremik had never had a single visitor out there, but would journey into the village once a month to visit the clockmakers' shops and drop off the beautiful hand-carved pieces he had completed. He had been making his monthly journey into Triberg when he died. Herman Schroeder, the butcher, had spotted Ivo slumped over the wheel of his truck alongside the road leading into Triberg while on his morning delivery route. They found three cuckoo clocks carefully wrapped in canvas on the front seat, each labeled with the name of the shop where they were destined.

Suddenly, the silence was interrupted by a loud bark. Stefan turned to check the crate in the back of his truck. *What am I going to do with him,* he wondered. He knew if he dropped the dog at the *Hundefänger,* he would surely be put down. After all, who would want to adopt a full grown, male boxer with nothing known of the dog's temperament or background? Was he friendly? Would he get along with other dogs? Would he accept a new master? Stefan knew of only one person who would care enough to take the time to help this dog and his thoughts turned to her. Maybe she'll finally say "yes" to me today, he thought happily.

As Stefan pulled into the driveway of the Triberg Municipal Office, his demeanor became serious. He was here on official business. He had a job to do. He scooped up the box containing the legal documents he'd found at the cabin and headed to the office door.

"Well, look who's here—Stefan Klein," said Anja, looking up from her typing to greet the handsome young man with the short-cropped, sandy-blonde hair and the smiling eyes.

Most people, including Stefan, thought Anja Wagner very pretty, though she did not seem to realize it or care. With a slight, athletic figure, and long, flowing light brown hair, which she simply pulled back in a barrette, she looked much younger then her twenty-two years. She had expressive, bright-blue eyes, and always greeted everyone with a warm and genuine smile. Stefan came through the door carrying the cardboard box, which he placed gently in front of her, grinning broadly in spite of his resolve.

"This is all I could find in the way of paperwork," he said with renewed seriousness. "There are a few more boxes in the truck—his wood carving tools, and anything else I thought his next of kin might want. Not much though. It seems he led a pretty simple life. Oh, there is one more thing. There's something on the truck I need help unloading."

"Will we need the cart?" Anja asked, rising from her desk and heading toward the storage closet.

"Good idea," he answered.

Anja pulled a heavy-duty cart out of the closet and passed it to Stefan, then threw on her coat as she headed toward the door. She was thinking she would have to do a search of the official records to find Ivo's next of kin. She knew the Bremik's had no children, but hopefully she could find some distant relative who would want these few possessions.

"Did you board up the cabin?" she asked as they started toward the truck.

"Yes," Stefan nodded.

Suddenly she stopped. "Why . . ." she asked, staring wide-eyed at the back of the truck, "is there steam coming from inside that crate?"

"That," said Stefan grinning, "would be from the dog."

"Dog?" she said, surprised. "And just what am I supposed to do with a dog?"

"I'm not sure," said Stefan. "But I think we both know what will happen to him if I take him to the Hundefänger. So I figured the crate is the personal property of Ivo Bremik and I was told to bring his property to this office. What's inside the crate is of no matter to me."

"Why Stefan Klien—I never would have pegged you for such a softy," she teased.

"Well," he muttered, "let's just say I'm repaying a long overdue debt."

"A debt?" she asked, curiously. "What kind of debt?"

He looked at her for a moment, then, raising his hands like threatening claws and speaking in a mock scary voice, he said, "He once saved me from a pack of ferocious wild dogs!"

"OK, so don't tell me," she said with a shrug.

Anja helped Stefan lower the heavy crate onto the cart. She held the door open as Stefan maneuvered it into the building. Anja knew the dog was not really her responsibility, but in her heart she knew that Stefan was right about the dog being put down. Anja had a soft spot for animals. Stefan had gambled on this and won. Yes, Anja would help this dog.

After he had finished unloading the few remaining boxes and lining them up neatly against the back wall of the small office, Stefan reached for a styrofoam cup and filled it with hot coffee. "You know—" he said with a sidelong glance, "that offer to take you out to dinner is still open."

"I know," she answered shyly, eyes down.

"Well, call me if you change your mind." He smiled and closed the door behind him as he headed back to work.

Anja turned her attention to the pressing matter at hand, a large but seemingly friendly male boxer. She knelt in front of the crate and the dog whined to be let out. It was obvious to her that he had been very well cared for. He had a radiant, silky coat, a clean healthy mouth and well-trimmed nails. She went back to the box on her desk and began her search for clues to some relative who might want to take the big dog. At the bottom of the box, her eyes fell upon a collection of aged scrapbooks. She pulled the top one out and slowly opened it, her curiosity now piqued. It was filled with a collection of articles clipped from old newspapers dating as far back as forty years. Beneath the scrapbooks was a stack of old magazines, yellowing with age. As she began reading the articles and studying the photos, she became aware for the first time that old Ivo Bremik was much more than a humble woodcarver.

Anja's eyes poured rapidly over the many papers and scrapbooks—story after story about Ivo, his dogs, and their remarkable accomplishments. Apparently his kennel "Von Bremik" had been famous across Europe. She found dozens of pictures of a much younger Ivo, with his late wife, Beata, at his side, smiling as they were being handed trophies, ribbons, awards and certificates.

In every photo they stood beside a stunning champion boxer posing majestically for the camera. *Wow*, she thought, *I had no idea.* It was becoming very clear to her that Ivo Bremik had been a well-known world-class breeder of boxers.

Anja dug deeper into the box and came upon a pedigree, the only one there. Though Anja did not know what all the letters and numbers appearing before and after the dogs names meant, she knew it had to be the pedigree for this dog. She looked at the front of the papers to check the date of birth. This pedigree was for a male about three-years-old. The age and description seemed to fit.

"So, my friend," she said, "If these are your papers, it appears your name is Bodo." The dog's ears perked up upon hearing his name and he now watched Anja with sharp anticipation. "Ah, so this *is* you! Well, Herr Bodo, now that we know your name, all I have to do is find you a home. But first, I'll bet you're hungry."

Anja opened the paper bag containing her lunch of a hardboiled egg, a hunk of black bread, a piece of cheese and a pickle. "Hmm, not much here for a hungry dog," she said. "But it will have to do for now."

Anja dropped the bread and the hardboiled egg through the top of the crate and watched as the dog seemed to inhale them, then turned back to the box on her desk to resume her search. She examined every paper, every envelope, anything that would give her a clue.

It was in a little stack of Christmas cards, tied neatly with a piece of twine, that she found what she was looking for. The cards, still in their colored envelopes, all had the same return address: The Jenkins Family, Gulfside Beach Florida, USA. Anja gently opened one of the cards. It read *"Dear Aunt Beata and Uncle Ivo."* Anja turned to her computer and the Internet. Since she now had their name and address, it was not difficult to acquire their phone number. Next she checked the time difference. Calling them in the middle of the night certainly would not help her cause. The time zone conversion chart showed it would be 6:30 A.M. in Florida, USA. A little early she thought, but at least it's not the middle of the night. She felt slightly uneasy at the thought of the sad news she was duty-bound to deliver. As she dialed the phone number, she silently hoped her English would be good enough.

CHAPTER TWO

BODO GOES TO AMERICA

Rodger Jenkins sat at the long trestle table his father had built over 30 years ago. Staring out of the bay window that faced toward the Gulf of Mexico he emptied his second cup of coffee. His hand passed gently over the wash-worn finish of the old table, and then unconsciously swept a lock of his jet-black hair back behind his ear. Rodger was forty-four, of medium height, very fit, and possessed the rugged patina of a man who had spent years on the ocean.

He enjoyed this time in the early morning when the house was silent. Soon the kids would be up and the day would begin. For now, he could sit and watch the early morning mist from the Gulf slowly drift inland, layer upon layer, until finally it vanished in the growing heat of Florida's morning sun. Rodger could see his neighbor, Benny, locking his door and turning toward the beach three blocks away. He was heading to breakfast at the Gulfside Grill, as he did every morning, then on to the shipyard to start the early shift.

But today would be different. Rodger looked down at the green piece of paper in front of him. It was a notice handed to each employee at the end of their shift yesterday informing them that, due to certain "unforeseeable financial pressures," Bravetti Marine would be closing at the end of the month. The news wasn't exactly a surprise. There had been rumors for weeks. Bravetti Marine was, or at least used to be, among the most respected builders of yachts and small pleasure boats on Florida's west coast. Sal Bravetti had founded it in 1922, soon after his arrival from Catania, Sicily, a sea-side village famous for its shipwright heritage. It began as a simple three-man operation committed to using the age-old skills and techniques of the long line of master boat-builders from which he descended. His dedication to his craft and his unmatched attention to detail would soon propel him into large-scale production. Bravetti Marine quickly grew into a major yacht and pleasure boat manufacturing center. After Sal passed away, his two sons carried on the tradition faithfully and brought production techniques and equipment well into the next century.

Then, four years ago, the Bravetti brothers decided to retire. With their advancing years, and not one of their children interested in carrying on the family business, they decided reluctantly the time to sell had come.

The highest bidder was an entrepreneur named Clinton Bozwell, a man with a questionable business reputation, but possessing the money. He assured the brothers it was his dream to carry on exactly as they would have wished and that he would be an excellent steward of the name. He pledged to do everything in his power to assure that "Bravetti" would forever be synonymous with excellence.

Rodger had worked as a foreman for the Bravetti brothers for fourteen years. The downhill spiral had begun almost the instant Bozwell took over. First came the cost-cutting. Materials were downgraded to the point of compromising structural integrity and safety.

Next, after orders began to fall off, had been the firings. Rodger had been forced to cut his men by almost a third, and worse, he had to be the one to let them go. It had sickened him to do it. The memory of the faces of longtime friends and family men, as he told them they no longer had jobs, still caused his stomach to retch. Rodger was certain that eventually there would be an accident. His fears were tragically proven correct two weeks ago. Just under the surface of the coastal waters of central Florida lay a multitude of obscured sandbars. A newly launched Bravetti craft with a family of six aboard had shattered after striking one.

The USCG Office of Boating Safety had immediately stepped in and halted the production of all watercraft until the completion of a full-scale investigation.

Rodger had repeatedly warned Bozwell that the extra expense of double-reinforcing the fiberglass hulls beyond national standards was vital for this part of the country. Bozwell simply sneered at him and threw him out of the office. Rodger thought about quitting every time he passed through those gates, but with a family to support and jobs scarce, he had no choice.

The accident was no surprise to him. Still, the shock of the closing of the largest employer in the small town of Gulfside Beach was going to be felt all along this section of the west coast of Central Florida. Rodger was staring blankly, watching his longtime friend disappear around the corner when the loud ring of the telephone startled him. He glanced at his watch. It was 6:35 A.M. He grabbed the receiver off the wall quickly to avoid waking the kids.

"Hello?" he said.

"Gud morning," said a woman's voice. *"My name is Anja Vagner und I am calling from ze location of Triberg, Germany."*

"Yes? " said Rodger, apprehensively.

"I am seeking to find ze family Yenkins," said the

woman.

"I'm Rodger *Jenkins*," said Rodger, pronouncing the "J".

"I am seeking ze family of Herr Ivo Bremik von Triberg."

Upon recognizing the name of his wife's old uncle from Germany, he responded, "I think you need to speak to my wife—please hold on while I get her."

As he started to lay down the phone, he saw Hannah already approaching, her short, blonde hair still tousled from sleep. As she tied the belt of her robe she gave him an apprehensive look.

"It's long distance from Germany." he whispered, handing her the receiver. "Something to do with your Uncle Ivo."

"Hello?" she said as she pulled out a chair and sat down. Rodger listened as Hannah began to speak to the woman in German.

Hannah's mother Elsa had come to America as a young bride and had never abandoned her native tongue. Rodger had always enjoyed listening to Hannah and her mother speaking German together, even though he didn't understand a word of it. He found the cadence and rhythm of the language fascinating. He sat watching his wife's face for some clue to what was being discussed. Hannah listened as Anja told her all she knew of the circumstances of her uncle's death and asked if she would be willing to accept delivery of his few personal effects.

They talked for several minutes, and after jotting notes down on a note pad, she hung up. Rodger got up from the table and returned carrying two mugs of hot coffee. He placed one in front of Hannah and sat down.

"My Uncle Ivo," she said, "died yesterday."

"I'm so sorry, Hannah," he said gently, knowing how hard she might take the news of losing another relative so soon after the death of her mother. Being an only child, Hannah and her mother had been extremely close.

"How did they find you?" he asked.

"The Christmas cards," she said. "They found them among his things. That was a woman from the municipal office. She said she also found a deed to a burial plot right next to where Aunt Beata was buried and that she would handle all the arrangements. She asked if she could send me his personal effects. Seems there's no one else. I told her yes, but Rodger, we need to talk about something important he left behind."

Rodger looked up curiously and tilted his head in interest, thinking how convenient even a small inheritance would be in light of his impending unemployment.

"Well," she began slowly, "it seems—Uncle Ivo—had

—a—a dog."

"A *what!*" said Rodger, his hopes of any kind of inheritance suddenly dashed. "What kind of dog?"

"A boxer," said Hannah, "A three-year-old male. If we don't want him, he'll be turned over to the local pound. Anja—the woman on the phone—thought she should try to find a relative to take him before resorting to that. She feels pretty certain he'd be put down, being full grown and all. She also said we wouldn't have to pay anything for shipping," Hannah added, reading her husband's mind. "Uncle Ivo had a few dollars set aside. She said even after the funeral expenses, there's still more than enough left over to cover the cost of paperwork, health certificates and air fare."

"Hannah," said Rodger, interrupting her. "Now wait. A dog is about the last thing we need right now, another mouth to feed and a big one at that. I don't know about this."

Hannah looked across the table at her husband. She knew he would need time to think it over. Rodger was not one to make spur-of-the-moment decisions. She needed no time at all. She had known instantly she wanted this dog. She knew it was sentimental, but the dog was probably the last link she had to her mother's family.

Rodger sensed Hannah wanted the dog and rolled his

eyes in resignation. "I suppose we can talk about it later," he said.

"I told Anja we would give her our answer tomorrow morning. Besides, I just think it would be good for the kids." She didn't say what she was really thinking, which was—*it would be good for the kids to have something to focus on other than their father losing his job.*

They sat there in silence for a few moments, each filled with their own thoughts. From the living room came the sound of a cuckoo clock chiming out seven o'clock and Hannah rose to wake the children.

Anja hung up the phone. "Well, big guy," she said out loud to the dog. "Nothing to do now but wait."

She rummaged through the boxes Stefan had neatly placed along the back wall until she found what she was looking for. She pulled a long leather leash out of one of the boxes. "I'll bet you could use a walk." Upon seeing the leash, the dog began to whine with anticipation. Anja opened the door to the crate just enough to reach in to attach the leash to his collar, but the eager dog had other ideas. In a flash, he exploded out of the crate. Anja was knocked flat by the force of the door. Panic flashed through her. She was completely unprepared for the amount of strength the dog possessed, and she really didn't know if he was friendly. Suddenly, with a leap, the dog was standing over her. She instinctively covered her face with her hands and rolled to her side. The dog responded by hopping over her body to get to her. Then she felt his cold wet nose trying to nudge her hands away. He's *playing*, she thought with an enormous sense of relief. To be certain, she slowly moved her hands aside and peeked at him. He instantly thumped his huge front paws down flat in front of her, wagging his entire body and whimpering. "You *are* playing," she said out loud. "Why you're nothing but a big baby!"

As she dropped her hands, he went wild licking her face. She covered her face again, but this time it was not out of fear.

Anja got up off the floor and gave the dog a vigorous head rub. His eyes never left her as she put on her coat, hooked him to the leash, and headed for the back door.

Rodger looked up from the piece of wood he had been turning over and over and staring at and saw Benny standing there.

"Hey, Rog—you listening?"

"Huh, oh, sorry, I must've been daydreaming."

"I said—Jerry heard that the plant over in Ocala might be taking on some of us. A few of us are going over there after our shift ends. You in?"

"Sorry Benny, I have to get home. Some stuff I need to do. Family stuff. But let me know how it goes."

"Sure thing," said Benny. "Well, see you tomorrow."

Rodger turned off the machine at his work station and walked to the time clock to punch out. As he passed through the shipyard gates to walk the three short blocks to his home, he pondered the phone call from Germany. He knew Hannah wanted the dog and he also knew that she was probably right about the kids.

It's just a dog, he thought, as he made his way past the small colorful bungalows that dotted this section of town. Who knows how long it will be before I can do something special for them again. Suddenly, a dog seemed like a very small thing to do for his family.

As a warm, peach-colored dawn gently settled over

Gulfside Beach, Rodger and Hannah sat down with their morning coffee waiting for the call from Germany.

They decided not to tell the children until they were certain. Hannah, an RN who worked part time at the Gulfside Manor nursing home, was reminding Rodger that she would be working on Saturday. "You know, I was talking to Shelly yesterday at lunch. You remember Shelly, don't you?"

"Shelly? Oh, yeah, the one married to the K-9 police officer, Mike O'Conner."

"Yes, that's her. Well anyway, she was telling me that she has a dog entered in a dog show this weekend, down at the fairgrounds."

"Do they have a boxer?" asked Rodger.

"Oh no, she has a wonderful little thing she calls an Iggy—an Italian Greyhound," said Hannah, "and we were thinking it might be fun for you and the kids to go. She said there would be boxers there. I think it would be exciting for the kids to actually see one in person."

"I'm kind of curious myself," said Rodger. "Maybe we can pick up a few pointers from the owners." Rodger had never owned a dog.

Right on schedule, as the cuckoo clock sounded the hour, the phone rang. Rodger and Hannah looked at each other as Hannah headed to the phone.

"Guten Tag," Hannah began, after hearing Anja's voice. Anja was anxious as she greeted Hannah. She was feeling dreadful about leaving the dog locked in his crate all night in the back room of the office. She had thought about sneaking him up to her second story walk-up for the night, but knew the landlord would be very angry if she broke the strict "no pets" rule.

"Have you made a decision?" she asked Hannah in German, holding her breath until she heard the answer.

"Ja, Anja," said Hannah. *"Wir sind glücklich, den Hund zu nehmen."*

"Oh, wunderbar!" exclaimed Anja.

They began discussing the details of shipping the dog to America. Rodger picked up the words "Stuttgart" and "Tampa."

"Well," Hannah said smiling as she hung up the phone. "Looks like we have a dog! Anja will try for a Saturday flight, which would get him to Tampa on Sunday. She'll e-mail us copies of his papers and all the details when she has them."

"So," said Rodger, "we have a dog. I guess we should tell the kids. By the way, did she happen to tell you his name?"

She turned to Rodger and beamed. "His name is Bodo," she said. "Bodo Von Bremik."

Hannah went to wake the children. "Alec Joseph, time to get up, let's go!"

"But Mom—" whined 14-year-old AJ as he pulled the covers over his head, "it's too *earrrrrly.*"

"C'mon, sleepy head. Your father and I have something important to tell you."

"Good morning, girls," said Hannah as she entered her daughters' room. Nixie, six-years-old and still very much the baby of the family, reached up for her mother's arms. Her oldest daughter, Becki, rolled over in half-sleep, her long red hair tangled across the pillow.

"What time is it, Mom?" she asked.

"Time to get up, honey. Daddy and I have some important news."

Anja had her work cut out for her. It would take her a few days to arrange the shipping. In addition to the stack of paperwork, she would have to get Bodo to a veterinarian for his health certificates and she would need to track down his medical records, which should not be too difficult since Triberg had only one vet.

Dr. Kohl's office was an easy walk for Anja from her office. As she and Bodo entered the small, tidy office, Dr. Kohl was just saying goodbye to an old woman with a very fat cat in her arms. After the woman left, he turned to Anja smiling, and glanced down at the dog. "Bodo! My friend," he said, with a surprised expression, which quickly turned to one of concern as Anja told him the news about Ivo and about the arrangements she had made for the dog. Anja was greatly relieved when Dr. Kohl asked if she needed a place to board Bodo until his flight on Saturday.

"Do the Americans know anything about this dog?" asked Dr. Kohl.

"Just what I could get from his papers. Is there anything in particular I should tell them?"

After a long pause, he let out a sigh. "Anja," he began, "Let me tell you something. I have seen thousands of dogs in my years of practice and I've treated some of the finest working dogs in all of southern Germany. On many occasions I've watched Herr Bremik putting Bodo through his paces and, Anja, I must tell you, I believe this dog to be one of the most magnificent animals I have ever seen. I certainly hope the Americans understand and appreciate the decades of dedication and hard work it took to produce a dog of this caliber."

"I had no idea," said Anja.

"Do you want to leave him with us now?" asked the Doctor.

"Could I bring him back after work?" she asked, reluctant to part with him so soon.

"Just drop him off anytime. Oh, by the way, has he been fed today?"

"Only a few bites of my lunch," answered Anja.

"Better take this along," said the doctor, handing her a sack of food. "It's his favorite. I order it in especially for Herr Bremik."

Anja thanked the doctor and headed back to the office. With Bodo curled up at her feet, she called the airlines and booked a Saturday flight out of Stuttgart. "Well, Bodo," she said as she reached down and rubbed his ear. "It looks like you're going to America. Now, there's just one more thing to figure out. How am I going to get you and your crate to Stuttgart? I'll need someone with a truck." Then, without hesitation she turned to the phone and called Stefan.

"Stefan? Hi, it's Anja. I've been thinking about your offer for dinner and I was wondering if it's still good? Great! Well, actually I was thinking about dinner in Stuttgart on Saturday? Terrific, oh, and by the way, could you pick me up in your truck?—Oh, because I just love a man who drives a truck," she said with a grin.

On Saturday morning Anja checked and rechecked every detail to make sure everything was in place for Bodo's flight to America. She had e-mailed the itinerary, along with Bodo's papers, to Hannah, and carefully taped up the few boxes of Ivo's personal effects to be shipped along with the dog. Then she had picked up Bodo from the vet. He was extremely excited to see her again and pranced happily all the way back to the office. He now lay curled up behind her desk as Anja sat on the floor beside him, his massive head resting gently in her lap. Stefan would be along shortly.

"Anyone here?" shouted Stefan, scanning the empty office as he entered.

"We're down here," said Anja.

"We?" said Stefan, getting his answer in a heartbeat as Bodo leaped up to frolic at his feet in greeting. "You still here?" he said as he rubbed the big dog's head.

"Actually," said Anja, dusting herself off. "He's about to go to a new home."

"Terrific! Who'd you talk into taking him?"

"I'll fill you in over dinner."

"Great, I'm starved. Are you ready to go?"

"Yes, but would you mind if we make a little stop first?"

"Sure, where?"

"The Stuttgart Airport."

He looked at her confused. "The airport?"

"That's right," she said, smiling down at the big dog. "Bodo has a plane to catch."

CHAPTER THREE

THE DOG SHOW

Saturday morning, the day of the dog show, the Jenkins family was gathered noisily around the breakfast table. AJ was very excited about the prospect of having a new dog. He had been begging for one for years. Today, he was up before dawn and ready to go, talking nonstop about all the things he wanted to teach it.

Becki had taken the news with an air of feigned disinterest, but Hannah knew better. Becki loved animals, but showing too much interest might tarnish her new grown-up demeanor. After all, she was almost seventeen.

Little Nixie had simply squealed with delight. The dog was only three, and she was six. *Finally someone little to play with*, she thought.

"I sure wish you could join us, Hannah," said Rodger.

"Me too," she answered. "Now remember, Shelly was saying they start the judging at nine o'clock and go alphabetically, so be sure to get there early. You don't want to miss the boxers."

"Do I *really* have to go?" whined Becki, as she drew her thick red hair into a ponytail to pass through the back of her baseball cap. "I wanted to go to the mall with Pam today."

"She just wants to see *Jeeeremeee,*" teased AJ.

"I do *not!*" she retorted angrily, "I couldn't care less about Jeremy Hanson."

"Cut it out, you two," said Hannah, sternly. "Now both of you help me clear the table so you can get going."

As they hurried out the door, she yelled, "Keep a sharp eye on Nixie. You know how she wanders."

Hannah watched as they pulled out of the driveway, and a lime green VW bug convertible with the top down pulled into the spot. The driver waved to her. It was her friend and co-worker, Terry Langley, picking her up for work. She hurried out the door and hopped into the car.

As they approached the fairgrounds, Rodger was surprised at the large number of cars in the parking area.

"I had no idea it would be this crowded," he said as he looked for a spot. After finding one, they all headed for the main entrance. They approached a table attended by two elderly women who looked exactly alike who were selling tickets.

"Good morning," said Rodger to the women. They smiled back at him.

"Is there a fee to enter?" he asked.

"Actually, this weekend is the opening of our show season, which we usually set aside as our unofficial practice shows," said the first woman.

"We only ask a donation for the club," said the other woman.

"No problem," said Rodger, as he handed her a few dollars.

"Do you have a dog?" asked the first woman.

"No," said Rodger.

"Yes!" shouted all three children.

"Well, which is it, yes or no?" asked the second woman.

"As of today we don't," said Rodger, "but in the morning we have a boxer arriving from Germany."

"Oh, congratulations!" said both women at once.

"And you'll be wanting to show it?" asked the first woman.

"Show it?" asked Rodger.

"Well, sure," said the woman, "I mean, assuming it's an eligible purebred."

"Well, from what I know, he comes with a pedigree, so I guess he is a purebred. But I wasn't thinking of showing him."

"How old is he?"

"He's three years old and *I'm* six!" announced Nixie proudly.

"Well, good for you!" said the first woman, smiling at Nixie. "It's really great fun and we have a special category in the afternoon for junior handlers," she said. "Perhaps one of the children . . ."

"*I'll* do it, Dad!" shouted AJ.

"No, *me!*" cried Nixie.

"Don't look at me," said Becki.

"Now hold on everyone," said Rodger, not liking the direction this conversation was taking. "I don't think you can just pick up a dog at the airport in the morning and expect to put him into a show ring in the afternoon."

"Oh, heavens," answered the second woman, "our handlers do it all the time!"

"Still, I don't know," said Rodger, "This is definitely something we would need to talk about first. We'll have to get back to you on it."

"That will be fine," said the second woman, as she handed the entry form to Rodger. "Tomorrow is our last unofficial show this season, and that's the one you would really need to be in."

"Remember," said the first woman. "It's just a practice show, but you'll get an idea of how your dog compares to the standard, and you'll learn how he acts in the show ring."

"We'll think about it," said Rodger, as he folded the paperwork and put it in his pocket. "Could you tell us where the boxers will be?"

"Boxers are in the working-dog class, starting in Ring Three at nine-thirty," said the second woman, pointing toward Ring Three.

Rodger thanked the women for their help and they all headed toward Ring Three.

As they approached the area, they saw them. Boxers were everywhere. Impressive and imposing, they stood like regal granite statues. They had elegant bodies, well-defined, sturdy and powerful, with smart-looking pointed upright ears. All possessed the signature stump tails that continuously wiggled back and forth, the only outward sign of the well-trained show dog's excitement.

"Wow!" said AJ. "Dad, look at them. Is our dog going to look like *that?*"

"I guess he will," answered Rodger.

"No, Daddy, our dog will be *little*," said Nixie, "he's only three-years-old. I'm gonna' be *bigger* than him!"

"Honey, I'm afraid it doesn't work like that for dogs," he said, getting down on his knee to explain it to Nixie.

"But Daddy, that's not fair. I want someone little to play with," she pouted.

"I'm sure Bodo will play with you, Nixie. We'll just have to wait and see what he likes to do."

"I want him to play dolls with me."

"He's not gonna' play stupid *dolls* with you!" snapped AJ.

Rodger intervened, "How about we just wait and see what Bodo has to say."

"So *there*," said Nixie.

Becki had been standing silently watching the dogs in the ring.

"What do you think, Becks?" Rodger asked, looking fondly at his daughter. She so resembled his own mother, red hair and all, that he felt a slight pang. She had died when he was quite young.

Becki answered in one of those rare little-girl moments, where she forgets how grown-up she's trying to be, "Oh Daddy, they're *wonderful!* I've never seen such beautiful dogs! Just look at them!"

They watched the events the entire day. Their excitement about the arrival of Bodo was mounting. AJ bought a book on boxers at the book table, and Becki bought Bodo a bright red bandanna. They rode home exhausted and excited about their newest family member's arrival in the morning.

Hannah greeted them at the door. "How was it?" she asked, glancing at Rodger as he carried in Nixie, who was half asleep.

"Aw, Mom, wait till you see them. *Look!*" said AJ, holding open his book to a double page spread of a champion brindle boxer standing regal and proud. "He's gonna' be awesome!" he said as he ran off to the living room to read his book.

"Daddy says I can play dolls with him if he wants to," mumbled Nixie, half asleep in her father's arms.

"Oh, Becki," Hannah shouted after her daughter as she bounded down the hall, "Pam called for you."

"Thanks, Mom," she yelled back, her voice trailing away as she darted to the nearest phone.

"Are you hungry?" she asked, giving Rodger a kiss.

"No. We filled up on corn dogs and funnel cake at the show," he said, as he went to put Nixie on the sofa.

"So, was it fun? Did the kids enjoy themselves?"

"I would say so," he answered in a whisper as he threw a cover over Nixie.

"Honey, I have to tell you—you were right about this whole dog thing. Even Becki is getting into it. And I've never seen AJ so excited about anything. You should have seen him concentrating on the dogs in the ring, watching every move, memorizing the commands. You won't believe this, but he actually wants to enter the dog in a show tomorrow."

"You're not serious? A dog show?—Really?—*AJ?*"

"I know, it's crazy, but he's dead serious about it. I didn't have the heart to tell him no."

"Hmmm, so you thought I could be the bad cop?" she teased. Then, after a moment, she turned and looked at Rodger. "You know what?" she said. "Maybe we should let him."

"Let him! Just like that! No practice, no training. Just pick up some strange dog at the airport and enter it in a dog show!"

"Well, first of all, it's not exactly a strange dog. It was Uncle Ivo's, and according to my mother's stories about him, 'he always had a dog at his side'. I'm quite sure he knew how to train it. And after all, it's just a dog show. What's the worst that could happen? If he wants to show off his new dog to the world, I say let him. Besides, it's a lot better than his sitting around playing video games all weekend. You know how hard we've been trying to get him interested in something. This may be just what we've been looking for."

"Hmm, I hadn't thought of all that," said Rodger,

seriously. "I guess you're right. It is just a dog show. What's the worst that could happen?"

Hannah woke the children for the big day. Rodger had left hours earlier for the airport. He and Benny had gone together in Benny's truck to pick up Bodo. Hannah was going over her list as she loaded the family van; a picnic basket filled with sandwiches, plates, forks, napkins, cups, a jug of iced tea, a few folding chairs, and camera.

"*A* leash! Mom, I'm gonna' need a leash!" shouted AJ, frantically. "What am I gonna' use for a leash!"

"Relax," said Becki tousling his mop of wavy dark hair. "They had tons of them for sale there. Crazy colors, braided ones, jewels stuck on them, I'll even buy it for you."

"Nothing girly or stupid," he said. "Get one like this," he added, pointing to a photo in his book.

Hannah found a parking spot on the grass under a stand of trees. AJ led the way, with papers in hand, to the registration table to register his dog for the Junior Handler event. As they approached the table, the same two women they'd met yesterday were there.

"Why, hello again," the first woman said, recognizing the children. "Did you get your dog?"

"Our Dad's picking him up right now," answered AJ proudly. "And I would like to enter the show."

"Oh, that's wonderful!" said the second woman. "Did you fill out the form?"

"Yes, Ma'am, here it is. And I have these," he said, as he pulled the copies of Bodo's papers from his back pocket.

"Excellent." She looked over the documents and added Bodo and AJ's names to the roster. "Now the junior handler event isn't until two o'clock, so you have plenty of time to prepare," she explained with a smile. "You'll do just fine. Just walk your dog around the ring and be sure to listen carefully to your judge's instructions. Each judge has his or her own way. That's really all there is to it. And don't forget to have fun. Good luck," she said as she handed him back his papers and entry card.

Hannah watched as her son with a very serious air, signed the forms and politely thanked the women. "All set?" she asked, barely hiding her pride.

"Yep."

"All right. Now let's go look at those boxers."

The wait for Rodger and Benny seemed like an eternity. Hannah set up the folding chairs by the ring where AJ would be showing and watched the events going on around her with Nixie. Becki had gone to the vendor area to buy AJ his leash and AJ went from ring to ring, eyes glued to the handlers as they performed. It was almost one-thirty when Hannah looked up to see Rodger strolling toward them grinning. They ran to greet him, all talking at once.

As the kids ran ahead toward Benny's truck, Rodger hung back a few paces and glanced at Hannah.

"What's wrong?" she asked suspiciously.

"Hannah," he started. "The dog . . ."

"What about the dog?"

"Well, he's not exactly what we were expecting."

"What do you mean?" she asked confused.

"Well, you better come see for yourself."

He quickened his stride to catch up with the kids. Benny was standing beside the open bed of the truck. On it was the large wooden crate. Rodger leaped up onto the bed and opened the door to the crate, reaching in to grab the dog by its collar.

AJ remembered the leash Becki had just bought him.

"Here Dad!" he said, tossing it up to Rodger, who caught it with one hand and reached in to hook it to the dog. As the family got it's first look at Bodo emerging from his crate and rising to his full height, they were speechless. What they saw standing there before them was not at all what they were expecting to see. Compared to the boxers they had been watching all morning, he seemed huge. Thick muscles bulged and rippled across his powerful frame. His chest was extremely broad and deep and he was red, not the tannish fawn color of the other boxers at the show. He had a much deeper russet tone. Instead of small alert and upright ears, Bodo's were large, long, and hanging straight down. They flopped loosely as he moved his massive head from side to side. He let out a colossal yawn, exposing a formidable set of bright-white teeth and powerful jaws.

AJ just stared up wide-eyed at the big red dog with the very large head and long, floppy ears.

"I'm afraid that's not all, son," Rodger said, as he jumped down off the truck bed, Bodo following him. It was what followed Bodo that really surprised them. Where he should have had a neat and sturdy proud stump, Bodo had a tail, an extremely long tail, whipping wildly from side to side. It was made even more obvious by the bright flash of a pure white tip. No, this was not exactly what they had been expecting.

The family stood there staring. They all had just assumed he would look exactly like the boxers at the show, elegant compact bodies with upright ears and short, perky, stump tails. Yet here he stood, this big red dog with natural ears hanging down, whipping his long tail back and forth. AJ just continued to stare, crestfallen. Rodger turned to thank Benny as he started up his truck to leave. Benny would take the crate and the other boxes back with him. Bodo would ride home without it. Then he handed the leash to AJ.

"Better give him a walk son," he said, "he's been in that crate a very long time." AJ dutifully led Bodo away to the designated area to answer nature's call, which he did without delay.

"I don't understand," said Hannah "are we sure he's a purebred? He just doesn't look quite right."

"Doesn't look right!" said Becki, watching them leave. "Mother, he's wonderful! Did you see how friendly he looks? I'm sure he was actually smiling! And those ears are much cuter than those little pointy things on those other dogs, and I love his color! I don't care what anyone says, I think he's the most wonderful dog here!"

Hannah smiled at how predictable her oldest daughter was. Becki, having been teased her entire life for her own red locks, can always be counted on to root for the underdog, she thought to herself and laughed out loud at the pun. "I think you may be right, Honey," she

45

said, "but I'm not so sure your brother will see it that way."

"Oh Mother, AJ just has to like him, I mean, we're all he has left. Can you imagine how heartbroken he is right now, not understanding why he's been taken so far away from his home, waiting for his master to come for him, wondering if he'll ever see him again? Oh, Mother, it's so sad I could cry."

Hannah lovingly put her arm around her daughter's shoulder as they turned to go. "I know, Honey. We'll just have to give him a little time."

At that moment the voice on the loud speaker was saying the words: *"Fawn adult male boxers. Junior handler event, Ring Seven."*

"That's us," said Hannah and they hurried back.

AJ heard it too. As he led Bodo back to the ring to take his place in line among the other handlers, he was very absorbed in the task of controlling the powerful dog and oblivious to the fact that people were staring. Onlookers whispered behind their hands and some fellow handlers just watched flabbergasted. In addition to the natural ears and tail, Bodo was different in other ways as well. He stood at least half-a-head taller than the largest males there. He had far more bone and substance and a much larger head. He was shorter in muzzle, with larger flews on both sides of his mouth. Not nearly as elegant as the other dogs, his conformation was massive and powerful. Well-defined muscles rippled as he moved. In addition to his unique deep-red color, his white markings, though similar, were far less pronounced. All the other males in line at the show were so similar they could have been littermates. Bodo, on the other hand, stood out like a sore thumb. A German boxer is a striking and impressive dog, but for this conformation type of dog show, he might as well have been a poodle, because that was about how much chance he had at winning.

And that's exactly what the mysterious stranger with the gray beard was thinking.

"Walk your dog slowly once around the ring, then stop in front of me," the judge instructed.

As AJ's turn approached, the family watched nervously. The big red dog was not cooperating. Anxious to romp about after his long confinement, he wandered restlessly from side-to-side whining while the other dogs stood perfectly still. AJ did his best to control him. As he finally approached the judge for his turn, Bodo suddenly yanked him out into the open space of the ring and began to pounce and whine, begging to be allowed to run. AJ tried to do exactly what he had seen the other handlers doing. "Heel!" he yelled, to no avail. Bodo pranced in circles around him. Then, without warning, leaped playfully high into the air, knocking AJ off his feet and dragging him across the ground like a toy sled.

Rodger immediately lunged for the edge of the fence and shouted, "*Bodooo!*" Upon hearing his name, the dog froze and AJ quickly unwound his aching arm from the leash. Bodo appeared to be looking for someone. He began to pace rapidly back and forth along the fence, whining, and then he simply leaped out of the ring. AJ, still lying flat on his face in the dirt, could not remember ever having been so humiliated. He thought he had the stupidest dog in the world and he hated him. Hannah pushed her way into the ring to see if AJ was hurt. He got up and ran past her, fighting hard against the tears. She quickly determined that the bulk of the damage was to his ego. She did not go after him.

Rodger had bolted after the dog with words like lawsuit, liability and massive property damage flashing through his mind. Bodo plowed like a run-away locomotive through startled crowds of spectators. He leaped in and out of the show rings in his path with ease and grace, leash trailing, upsetting dogs and handlers alike. He raced through the picnic area, sailing high over table after table like a track runner doing hurdles, while frightened picnickers dove for cover. In his wake of destruction were overturned benches and tables, women clutching their children, a chorus of every dog on the premises barking and howling and the entire Jenkins family in hot pursuit.

The stranger had been watching everything with a calm and detached air. In fact, he had not taken his eyes off the dog from the moment he noticed him. As the convoy of flying red fur and hysterical humans raced toward him for the third time, he decided he must act. Perhaps he was wrong but—*No!* he thought, *I am certain!* And with the complete confidence of a man who has spent a lifetime handling dogs, he boldly stepped directly into the path of the oncoming boxer. Facing the animal now bearing down on him, he snapped up his arm and shouted, "*Plaaaatz!*"

To the amazement of everyone watching, the airborne dog dropped flat to the ground and froze.

Silence spread through the crowd. All eyes were on

the man. Bodo layed there as rigid as a statue. The man then strolled calmly past the dog through the parting crowd toward Hannah, Rodger and AJ, who stood hunched over, gasping to catch their breath, and staring in grateful amazement.

"I can't believe I didn't think of it," said Hannah, between breaths. "He only understands *German!*"

The man approached them. "Des is your dog, yes?"

"Yes," they answered breathlessly, Hannah's ear catching the thick German accent.

"Pleaze allow me to introduce myself." Bowing smartly, he said, "I am Herr Viktor Vilhelm Adler of Emden, Germany, at your service."

"Ich bin Hannah Jenkins und das ist mein Ehemann Rodger," said Hannah, extending her still trembling hand to the man.

"Sie sprechen Deutsch!" he responded delightedly, taking her hand in his. Then turning to Rodger with his hand outstretched, *"Guter Tag, Sir!"*

"Sorry," said Rodger, shaking the outstretched hand, "I'm afraid I don't speak German. But I'm very pleased to meet you."

"Ah, vell, than ve shall use ze English."

"These are my children," said Hannah, turning to look for them, "Becki, Nixie and AJ."

"Ahh yes, AJ, ze young man I see in ze ring."

AJ hung his head in embarrassment at the reminder.

"Ach, never mind," said Viktor. "Dat vas really quite an exciting show. Und for zis I must thank you," he said bowing again as he extended his hand to AJ, who sheepishly grinned and took it. "Und now, pleaze, to tell me who ve have here," he asked, strolling back toward Bodo, who had not moved a whisker.

"That's Bodo," said Hannah. "Our new dog."

"Very new," said Rodger. "He just arrived this morning from Germany."

"Humph," said the tall, well-built, middle-aged man. As he walked in a circle around the dog, he slowly stroked his neatly trimmed beard. It was not difficult to understand why Bodo had obeyed him. There was an unmistakable air of authority surrounding the man. It was quite obvious that he was used to giving orders and having them obeyed.

"Young man," he said turning to AJ, "please to valk your dog around a little bit for me."

The curious crowd, still hanging around to see what would happen next, moved back a little to give the boy some room. AJ picked up the dangling leash and tugged hard. Bodo didn't budge. AJ looked up at the man for help.

"Oh, yes, yes, sorry. Please to hand me zat paper in

your pocket." AJ handed him his show brochure. Viktor produced a pen from his breast pocket and wrote a few words on it and handed it back to AJ. "Now, you must listen very carefully to me und do exactly as I tell you, understand?" AJ nodded. "I vant you to look directly at your dog and say each vord, vone at a time in ze firm voice."

"Now?" asked AJ.

"Yes, yes, now," said the impatient German. AJ looked at the first word, then looked at Bodo who was watching him with great attentiveness.

"Steh!" AJ said firmly. Bodo quickly rose up to a standing position. AJ's face lit up.

"More! Do ze others," said Viktor, motioning with his hand to keep going.

AJ read the next word, "Platz!" he said, and Bodo instantly dropped back down to the ground, his eyes now locked on AJ.

"Continue!"

"Sitz!" AJ said, and Bodo rose up to a sitting position.

"Und ze next vord," said Viktor.

"Geblaut!"

Bodo snapped out a deep, thunderous bark at AJ, who stumbled backwards startled.

"Again," said Viktor.

AJ regained his composure quickly and tried again.

"Geblaut!" Bodo barked again.

"Und now ze last vord is ze vord for *heel*. You must stand here beside him and say ze vord as you step out vith ze left foot."

AJ walked around to stand where Viktor pointed. "Fuss!" he shouted, stepping out with confidence, and Bodo did. AJ walked away bursting with pride, as the crowd of onlookers let out a cheer, clapping as he walked past them, head held high, the big powerful dog finally at heel.

It was very obvious to every experienced breeder, handler and judge present in the crowd that day that this dog was extremely well trained as a working dog, not a show dog.

As AJ led Bodo away, Viktor watched them closely. He trailed behind them to study the back movement, moved to the side, then walked hurriedly to the front and stopped to examine his forward movement. He said nothing, but simply nodded his head.

"I wonder what he's up to?" Rodger asked Hannah.

"I don't know, but he certainly does seem to know his way around dogs."

Viktor finished his assessment and returned to Hannah and Rodger. "Please, may I offer you some refreshment?" he asked, nodding toward the food vendor tent where they were still putting the tables and benches back up following Bodo's rampage. "And please bring ze boy."

"Go ahead, Mom," said Becki, taking Nixie's hand. "We'll be OK."

They sat around a picnic table under a large tent. Rodger came carrying three coffees and a lemonade for AJ. They exchanged a few pleasantries and Viktor began to tell them about himself. He is considered a hobby-type breeder of boxers in Germany. He was in town on business and decided to take in the show to get a first hand look at the American-style boxer.

After finishing his introduction, Viktor, with typical German bluntness, blurted out one of the questions that had perplexed him since first laying eyes on this dog. "Please to forgive my bad manners, but I really must know how is it possible zat a family all ze vay here in America, knowing nothing about ze European boxer, has in zeir possession such a magnificent specimen of a purebred German dog?" Meanwhile he was wondering why this dog seemed so familiar.

"Well," Rodger began. "We inherited him from my wife's uncle, who passed away just last week. The German authorities arranged for us to take him in, so he wouldn't be sent to a pound. It seems there was no one else. My son got it in his head to enter him in the show today to see how he would do," he said patting AJ on the back.

"Und do you know from whom your uncle acquired such a magnificent dog?"

"Oh, he had kept and bred dogs his whole life," said Hannah. "I'm fairly certain he bred the dog himself."

"Und vhere vas your uncle from?"

"Triberg."

"Triberg," said Viktor, "ze small village in ze Black Forest?"

"Yes," said Rodger," that's the one."

"Bah, zis cannot be," said Viktor, shaking his head from side to side. "I know every breeder of ze boxer in all of southern Germany und zere are none anyvhere near Triberg. You must be making ze mistake. Ze kennel zat bred a dog of zis superior quality would be known everyvhere in Germany und by me certainly!"

"But, the gal in the Baden-Württemberg office sent us copies of his papers," said Hannah.

"Zen she sent ze *wrong* papers," Viktor insisted stubbornly, dismissing the thought with an abrupt wave of his hand.

"But," continued Hannah, "she sent us all the papers they found in Uncle Ivo's desk, and he . . ."

Viktor's head snapped toward Hannah. "Please," he asked, eyes flashing, "tell me, vhat vas ze family name of zis Uncle Ivo?"

"Why it's Bremik," replied Hannah. "Ivo Bremik."

Upon hearing that, Viktor bolted straight up out of his seat.

"Madame, are you informing me zat Herr Ivo Bremik of ze Kennel Von Bremik, ze most well-known breeder of boxers in all of Europe, is . . . er, vas, your uncle?"

"I didn't know all that about the dogs, but yes, that would be my uncle, unless there are two Ivo Bremiks."

"Was zis uncle married to a lovely und kind voman called Beata?" he asked.

"That's right!" said Hannah, surprised. "But Aunt Beata passed away about six years ago."

"Madame," said Viktor bowing very deeply from the waist to Hannah, "Please allow me to offer you my deepest condolences on ze loss of both your aunt und your uncle. I vas acquainted vith them."

"You knew them?"

Viktor nodded solemnly, "I did, und it is a great honor for me zis day to meet ze family of such a vonderful couple."

"Thank you so much. Now you must tell me everything. Please sit down," said Hannah.

"Und now," said Viktor returning to his seat, "I am understanding everyzing." Looking down at Bodo who lay quietly at AJ's feet he said, "Zis," his open hand pointing to Bodo, "is a Von Bremik dog!"

"Yes, he is!" said AJ wide-eyed as he produced the crumpled papers from his back pocket. "That's exactly what it says here! See!" He handed them to Viktor, who read in silence, muttering to no one in particular.

"Ahh, yes, yes," he said, pointing to a name on the pedigree. "I knew vell ze grandsire of Bodo, Cuno Von Bremik. He vas vone of ze finest boxers ever produced in all of Germany, und he excelled in the sport of Schutzhund. I had never seen such a dog as zis. I vill never forget him. To watch him work was a thing of beauty. Zuch power und grace. I do not know zis son of Cuno, Falco Von Bremik, but according to zis, Herr Bremik must have bred him vhen he vas quite old. Zere vere only two offsprink in zis last litter, a very small litter, but not unusual from an old sire. There vas zis male pup, Herr Bodo, und it appears he has a sister. Vhere is zis sister?" Viktor asked abruptly.

"We don't know anything about a female," said Hannah. "We were only told about Bodo."

Viktor put down the papers, still trying to sort it out. "Now I know vhy I can not take my eyes off zis dog. It vas ze grandsire I see in ze grandson!"

Viktor went on to say that when he was new to the boxer world, he would often see Ivo and his lovely wife Beata at many Schutzhund trials and dog shows. He was always impressed by the consistently high caliber of their dogs. Wherever they competed, they always had a dog or two in the highest scores, or in the top-rated winners group.

Pointing to a name on the pedigree, he reminisced, "Ze day zis dog, Cuno Von Bremik von his Schutzhund 3 title vas ze last time I vas ever to see Herr Bremik. I had heard he sold off most of his dogs, und moved to ze country to retire. I never heard nor read of him again. Now I learn zis dog comes from ze Black Forest und ze pieces of ze puzzle are together."

"So you were familiar with Uncle Ivo's dogs?" asked AJ, wanting to hear more.

"Familiar!" snapped Viktor. "Of course I vas familiar. Every breeder in Europe vas familiar vith ze Kennel Von Bremik! Zere is not a kennel in Germany zat does not have ze Von Bremik line somevhere in zeir pedigrees."

He spoke with pride as he described the dogs in the pedigree that he personally saw compete at trials. He then pointed out the names of the dogs that also appeared in his own champion bloodline. "Zis is a very important bloodline und one zat needs to be preserved!" Viktor said sternly. "Un animal like zis is surely vasted here in America. If he vere in Germany, he could have his pick of top breeders to live vith und be bred to females from all over Europe to preserve zis line Herr Bremik spent his entire life perfecting." Viktor stopped his rambling and lowered his head. "I meant no insult to your family, or country, it's just zat . . ."

"Never mind," said Rodger. "We understand."

"Mister Adler?" asked AJ, breaking the silence. "What is Schutzhund?"

Viktor thought for a few moments, thinking of the correct words to explain this to AJ with his limited English. "Schutzhund," began Viktor, "is a German vord zat translates to protection dog."

Viktor then went on to explain as carefully as he could, the many complexities of Schutzhund training. He explained that the roots of the sport reach back more then one hundred years. It was originally developed for the German Shepherd, but was quickly adopted by breeders of other working dogs. Schutzhund was designed to be the ultimate test for working ability, a vital tool for breeders. By competing in Schutzhund trials, the working abilities of dogs could be determined, enabling breeders to test their breeding programs and help them reach their goals of breeding the best working dogs possible. Schutzhund is divided into three distinct areas.

The first area is tracking, where the dog must follow a course of footsteps using only scent. The course requires direction changes and along the course, the dog must locate several objects that were dropped and indicate their location to the handler. All the while, the dog is being judged for accuracy and determination.

The second area is obedience. Here the dog is put through a series of commands in a very large field. There will be heeling, both on and off leash, sit, down and stand. Also, some commands are given while the dog is moving. Part of the obedience requires the work to be done under the sound of a fired gun to test the dog's reaction and weed out any gun-shyness or fear of loud noises.

The final area in Schutzhund is protection, the part that most concerned Viktor about this dog. The protection phase is designed to test the dog's physical strength, agility and courage. It requires the handler to instill absolute control over the dog, which Viktor realized this family did not possess. During this phase in the trial, the dog will search hiding places for a hidden person, locate the person and guard them until the handler approaches. If this person tries to run or attack the handler, the dog must attack with a full, hard bite without hesitation. After the dog passes all three parts at a

Schutzhund trial before a judge, it is awarded the title of Schutzhund 1. This is a tremendous accomplishment noted by the designation *SchH1*, which will appear after his or her name from that day forward.

As the dog progresses in its training, and if the dog passes the next level of all three parts at a trial, it will be awarded Schutzhund 2. If the dog has the ability, and again passes the most advanced tracking, obedience and protection phases at a trial, the dog is awarded the highest level of Schutzhund possible—Schutzhund 3.

"You must understand," said Viktor, "dat zis is a very basic overview. Schutzhund is far more complex zan zis, but I vant to give you ze basic understanding."

"Wooooow," said Rodger, "I had no idea."

By this time Becki had returned with Nixie, who was getting tired and wanted her mother. She had been listening spellbound to what Viktor was saying.

"Can Bodo do all that?" she asked.

Viktor picked up Bodo's papers and began to read them. "Bodo has no Schutzhund title after his name, but if I know Herr Bremik, I am certain he is as vell trained as any Schutzhund 3 dog. Zee here, und here," he said, pointing out all the Schutzhund 3 titles in the pedigree. "Herr Bremik vas ze best Schutzhund trainer I have ever known."

"Mr. Adler," asked AJ, "I was wondering, when you saw Bodo running around the show grounds, how did you know he was a German dog?"

"Ah," answered Viktor with a wink, "I know ze German dog ven I see vone. Of course ze natural ears und tail are revealing, but it is ze *body* type of ze German boxer zat is most distinctive. I vould recognize one anyvhere. But, my young friend, it vas not just ze *vord* he obeyed, it vas ze attitude. Bodo vould have obeyed me in any language simply because I expected him to. You see, it is ze nature of all dogs to obey ze leader. A dog alvays knows who is, und who is *not,* ze boss."

Viktor then explained how in Germany, where the boxer breed began, ear-cropping and tail-docking have been banned. Europeans still breed for a sturdier, thicker, more muscular type of working dog, closer to the origins of the breed. In America, breeders have chosen to strive for a much more refined, lighter and elegant dog. This is not saying one type is better than the other, just different. Bodo is an excellent example of all the traits prized by German breeders.

Viktor looked over at the sleeping child in Hannah's arms and rose to go. "I have taken up too much of your afternoon. I should be going."

"Mr. Adler," asked Hannah. "How long will you be

in town?"

"I leave for Germany next Sunday."

"Well, would you do us the honor of joining us for dinner one night before you leave?"

"Ah, Madam, the honor vould be all mine!"

"Oh, wunderbar! There is so much I want to know about my aunt and uncle and besides, it's so nice to have someone to speak German with again."

"Again?"

"Not since my mother—"

"I am so sorry. Ve shall have ze nice long talk in German und I vill answer all your questions. I am staying at ze Gulfside Beach Inn. You may leave me ze message zere if you vish."

"We'll be in touch, and thank you so much for everything, Mr. Adler."

"Agh, please to call me Viktor."

"Well, thank you Viktor."

Rising to go, Viktor turned to Rodger and said, "Vould you und your son mind to accompany me to my automobile?"

"Sure." said Rodger.

As they walked to the parking lot together, it was Viktor who spoke first. "I am vishing to impress somezing upon you, but I did not vish to frighten your lovely vife."

"What is it?" asked Rodger concerned.

"I feel zat it is my duty to Herr Bremik and his family to be sure you appreciate fully ze huge responsibility zat comes vit owning a dog such as zis."

Viktor turned his full attention to AJ, and with great seriousness told him, "Zis dog, young man, iz more dog zen you can ever imagine. If you vish to be his master you must learn to control him at all times und under all possible circumstances. Remember, he has been trained in protection. A dog like zis carries a great amount of responsibility. You must learn everyzing you can about Schutzhund. Und if possible, you must find a club to join. Zere are a few hundred thouzand people around ze world who participate in Schutzhund. Zere must be a small club near here. Und you must be able to speak to Bodo in his own language at first. You must understand zat vhen Bodo accepts you und your family as his own, he vill take it upon himself to protect you, to guard your home und property, und if necessary, to give his very life in doing so. He has been bred and trained his entire life to do no less. Do you understand?" Viktor asked, looking directly at AJ.

"Yes, Sir, I do," AJ answered seriously.

Rodger and AJ waved goodbye to Viktor. They met up with Hannah and the girls and they soon left. Bodo, sporting his new red bandanna, staked out the back seat of the van and stretched out to sleep. AJ did not say much on the way home. He was thinking about everything Viktor had told him. He was determined to learn everything he possibly could about Schutzhund, just as he had promised Viktor.

Bodo meets an American boxer.

CHAPTER FOUR

The Cookout

Hannah handed the magnifying glass and the old photo to Rodger. "I can't believe it. Who does that look like to you?" Rodger moved toward better light. The black-and-white photo was of a bride and groom. The man was standing and the woman was sitting in front of him on a chair with a solemn expression. In the foreground stood a little girl of about six years, holding a skimpy bouquet of flowers. The girl had a slight smile.

"Whoa," said Rodger. "It's Nixie!"

"It's my mother," said Hannah, smiling. "That must be the day Uncle Ivo and Aunt Beata were married."

It was almost ten o'clock. The events of the day had exhausted the children and they had been sent to bed early. The dog had settled down for the night on a makeshift bed in the far corner of the living room, alongside the unused fireplace. Hannah and Rodger were on the sofa, going through the boxes of Uncle Ivo's things, which had arrived along with the dog. Rodger finished going through a box of old, well-used carving tools. After putting it aside he picked up another, which contained a tangle of leather and buckles. "Looks like some kind of harness," said Rodger, holding it up and trying to figure it out. There were also other dog-related items, including wooden dumbbells, leashes and collars. Hannah opened another box. "Honey, look at this!" she said as she came upon the old scrapbooks. "Wow, Viktor was right!"

As she sat there quietly reading, the cuckoo clock began to strike the hour, but they did not hear it. The dog, which had been sleeping quietly, suddenly jumped to his feet and began pacing rapidly around the room, whining. "Maybe he needs another walk?" asked Hannah.

"I'll take him out again," said Rodger, reaching into the nearby box for a leash.

While they were gone, Hannah continued to read. The articles fascinated her, and the photos of the beautiful champion German boxers were giving her a new understanding of the differences between the German boxer and the ones she had seen at the show. Bodo was definitely an extraordinary dog as compared to the champions in the photos. He was everything these dogs were and more. Even with her untrained eye, she was beginning to see what Viktor had so quickly detected. There was unquestionably something extraordinary about Bodo. Rodger returned, and after settling the dog in his bed, rejoined Hannah.

"It's so odd," said Hannah. "To see an entire lifetime reduced to a few cardboard boxes."

"A few boxes and a dog," said Rodger, looking over at the sleeping Bodo.

As the hour approached eleven, Hannah began straightening the stacks of papers to get ready to turn in. "I'll stay up a little while," said Rodger, engrossed in a magazine from 1962.

"OK. Well goodni . . ." For the second time that evening, the dog jumped up from a sound sleep and began to pace and cry. "What's wrong with him?" asked Rodger, confused.

"I don't know," answered Hannah. "But I guess you better walk him again. Maybe he's sick from the trip. He did eat a lot, maybe the new food?"

"All right," said Rodger. "Let's go Bodo."

When they returned, Hannah had gone to bed. Rodger settled the dog in his corner once more. He sat down and picked up the stack of old photos. As he worked his way slowly through the pile, pondering the faces of these strangers from another time, he eventually came upon one that he couldn't wait to show Hannah. It was a photo of Ivo and Beata taken in front of a large open fireplace in a living room of what he guessed was an old farmhouse. It was what he spotted on the wall beside the mantle that caught his eye. It was Hannah's mother's clock, the same clock that now hung on his living room wall! Hannah had owned it since the death of her mother, two years ago. Her mother had treasured it dearly from the moment it arrived from Germany. Uncle Ivo had made it as a wedding gift for Beata the year they were married.

The magical clock that looked like a tiny Swiss chalet had fascinated little Elsa. The clock face was encircled with delicately carved oak leaves, miniature pine cones, and at the base there was a little carved squirrel holding an acorn. Elsa would scurry from wherever she was to watch the little bird pop out of the mysterious door to sing out the hour.

Beata had never forgotten. She had told Ivo repeatedly that the clock was to go to her sister Elsa should anything happen to her. He looked up from the photo to the clock. There was no mistaking it. The hands on his clock said twelve. He waited for the little cuckoo bird that was about to appear. As it did, it happened again. The dog was up, crying and pacing.

"Of course!" said Rodger out loud, smacking his forehead, "It's the clock! Ivo built cuckoo clocks! He knows the sound of his master's work!"

He waited for the clock to finish it's clanging, then went over to the dog and he knelt down to comfort the animal, speaking gently to him. "You miss him ole boy, don't you? I'm sorry, boy, but there's not much we can do about it. But don't worry, in time, I think you'll come to like it here. We're not so bad."

The dog quieted down and nuzzled into Rodger's chest.

"Now how do you propose we get you through this night old boy?" he asked. "Obviously, I can't leave you here with the clock."

He thought of, and then quickly rejected, his own room. Rodger then decided AJ's room would be the best place.

"C'mon, boy," he said, heading down the hall. He quietly opened the door and led the dog in. Bodo knew exactly what a bed was for and gently climbed up and settled on his belly alongside the sleeping boy. He put his big head down on his front paws and sighed. Rodger closed the door quietly and went to bed.

As the early morning sun streamed through the open

window, AJ rolled over and opened his eyes. Beside him lay Bodo, belly-up, his head and long ears hanging straight down over the side of the bed. His flews draped wide open by gravity, as if he were caught in a wind tunnel, fully exposing teeth and gums, and his tongue dangled to one side. AJ thought he was dead. "Bodo!" he shouted. The dog opened his eyes and lifted his big head. AJ was delighted that his new dog was not dead.

"Good morning honey," said Hannah, frowning, as she shuffled to the table in her robe. "Rodger, I'm really concerned about AJ. Did you hear that awful snoring coming from his room last night? I think he may need his adenoids removed."

"Relax honey," said Rodger, laughing as he kissed her good morning. "It wasn't AJ, it was Bodo."

Rodger had, in fact, heard the strange noise too and leaped out of bed to investigate. As he neared the source of the mysterious racket, he remembered the dog. Opening the door to his son's room, he saw AJ sleeping soundly next to Bodo, who stopped his earsplitting snoring for a moment to look up at Rodger. He closed the door quietly and walked back to bed amazed at how soundly his son could sleep, and that a dog could actually snore.

"How did he get in AJ's room?" asked Hannah.

"I had to put him in there because of the clock."

"What clock?"

"The cuckoo clock."

"Rodger, I think I need a cup of coffee first. I don't know what you're talking about."

Rodger handed her the mug and began to explain what he had figured out. "It was exactly on the hour each time, remember?"

"What was?"

Rodger explained what had happened after she had gone to bed last night.

"Now that you mention it, I think you're right. It was on the hour— but I'm not sure I ever would have figured it out," said Hannah, sipping her coffee.

"Well, actually, I had a little help," he said rising to fetch the photo.

"I was looking at this when I saw it."

"Saw what?"

"Look. On the wall beside the mantle."

She spotted it. "Mother's clock!"

"That's right," he grinned. "I was looking back and forth from the photo to the clock, you know, comparing them, when the clock began to cuckoo and it happened again. He started crying and whining and it dawned on me. He associates the sound of a cuckoo clock with Uncle Ivo."

"Why, that makes perfect sense!" said Hannah, pondering. "Hmm . . . he better not make me choose between him and my clock," she joked.

Rodger wondered for a moment which one would win. "He'll get used to it in no time, I'm sure."

"He'd better."

AJ came to the breakfast table dressed for school and smiling, Bodo at his side.

"Good morning," said Hannah. "How'd you two sleep?"

"Great," said AJ, reaching for the box of cereal. "Don't you think Bodo may need a walk first?" asked Rodger.

"Oh, I forgot," said AJ, jumping out of his seat to grab the leash, Bodo following.

"And hurry back or you'll be late for school!"

Hannah closed the door behind them as they all left for the day. After cleaning up the kitchen and living room and trying to make neat the makeshift pile of old blankets they had hastily put down for Bodo, she decided he should have a proper bed.

Hannah loaded Bodo into the van, and they drove to

the local pet store. She parked the van, hooked Bodo to his leash and marched through the front door proudly.

"Hi, can I help you?" asked the young clerk whose nametag said "Sandy."

"Yes, I'm looking for a dog bed. A *big* one," she said, nodding toward Bodo.

The girl led her to the dog beds and began to explain all the pros and cons of the various models. Hannah, overwhelmed, decided Bodo should make the decision.

After they lined up all the models large enough to accommodate him, Hannah unhooked his leash. *"Komm Bodo, Leg Dich hin,"* she said, catching the puzzled look on the clerk's face from the corner of her eye. Bodo walked over to the line-up of beds, thoroughly sniffed each one, then climbed in and out of a few before finally circling around and dropping down on the one that looked like a giant floppy beanbag chair.

It was the least attractive from a decorating standpoint, sitting there among beautifully upholstered, fleece-lined, and leather-trimmed models, including one that resembled a little fold-open sofa.

"Hmmm," Hannah said. "It's not exactly the one I would have chosen." Then, turning to the clerk smiling, she said "We'll take it."

Over the next few days Bodo began to settle

comfortably into the family's routine. He spent his days following Hannah around the house when she was not at work, or on his new bed in the living room, waiting for AJ to come home.

On Thursday, at breakfast Hannah reminded Rodger about the invitation they had extended to Viktor. "How about a cookout on Saturday?" She asked.

"Sounds good to me," said Rodger.

"Great, I'll call Viktor's hotel today."

To Hannah's delight, Saturday was a perfect day, eighty-two degrees, clear and breezy.

Just as Rodger finished lighting the grill and Becki was smoothing the clean, white table cover over the battered picnic table, the rental car pulled up. Hannah quickly rinsed her hands of the fruit salad she was preparing and ran to greet Viktor.

"Hello," she said in German. "I'm so pleased you came."

Viktor looked as distinguished as the first time they'd met. He appeared impeccable in a crisp, starched white, short-sleeved shirt and khaki pants, only this time he carried in his hand an elegant cane. He also had a navy blue jacket carefully slung over one arm, and he wore a captain's hat. It was a white hat with a black band, with lush gold braid encircling the band and peak and it was emblazoned with an elaborate crest. His grey-blonde beard and full moustache with turned up ends gave him the unmistakable look of a sea captain.

"I am so pleased you remembered," he responded in German, tipping his hat. "Und zis iz for you."

From under his jacket he produced a bottle of wine. It was a Riesling wine from the famous Rheingau region near the Rhine River, home of some of the world's oldest wine-growing families. Hannah knew very little about wine, but decided it must be very special and acted accordingly.

"Oh, Viktor, you shouldn't have!" she said, as she looked at the label.

"Ach, it iz nothing."

As they turned to go in, AJ was just rounding the corner on his bike, returning from the market with some last minute items. Bodo was at his side. Upon seeing Viktor, the big dog bounded ahead to greet him.

"Herr Bodo, my old friend!" he said as the big dog jumped up on him.

"Nein!" shouted AJ as he rolled his bike to a stop.

Bodo obeyed immediately and got down off Viktor.

"I zee you have been learning," said Viktor as he ruffled Bodo's head.

"Yes, sir," said AJ proudly, handing the bag to Hannah as he walked his bike to its resting place.

"Wunderbar!" said Viktor as they all went inside.

The afternoon passed quickly. The family sat around the torch-lit picnic table with their guest, finishing their dinner and enjoying each others company as darkness slowly fell around them.

AJ told Viktor about his research on Schutzhund. He had located a club, just as Viktor had suggested and he and Rodger were scheduled to begin training next week.

The club was two towns away and had a large open field where they worked with the dogs.

Viktor nodded approvingly, thinking to himself, *it's you and your father who will be getting trained. Bodo already knows what to do.*

Viktor was very happy the family had taken his warning to heart. Only now would they begin to understand the real meaning of Schutzhund and to appreciate the hard work of Herr Ivo Bremik.

They dined on grilled salmon, vegetable kabobs and German potato salad—Hannah's mother's recipe—and of course, Viktor's marvelous wine.

Eventually the conversation came around to the shipyard.

"I have zeen it zo many times," said Viktor, shaking his head. "Putting profit before quality und safety und zen ze successful business iz ruined for ze future generations by stupidity und greed."

They also learned many fascinating things about Viktor. He hailed from the German harbor town of Emden, located at the mouth of the Ems River.

"Emden," Viktor explained, "has been a major port town since at least ze tenth century for ze ships heading to und from ze North Sea."

The Adler family owns and operates a large fleet of fishing vessels and is one of the areas largest exporters of herring, mussels and shrimp.

His family had been in the fishing business since the 1840s and Viktor had traveled the world and spoke many languages fluently, and of course, he loves boxers.

The dinner had been perfect. As things began to wind down, Hannah decided that the time was right and finally asked, "Are we ready for coffee and dessert?"

"Absolutely!" came the unanimous and eager reply.

Hannah had prepared a special dessert. It was her Aunt Beata's recipe, which she had discovered among Ivo's things. She had heard many times from her mother that Aunt Beata's Black Forest cake was the best in all of Triberg. She hoped she had translated the measurements and ingredients correctly. Hannah had worked on it late into the night. She had a little difficulty finding one ingredient called kirschwasser, until an old German woman at the supermarket told her what it was. She then set off for the liquor store to purchase the exotic cherry brandy.

The cake was comprised of three layers of chocolate sponge cake, each covered with whipped cream, cherry juice and sour cherries, then stacked high. The entire cake was covered with a thick whipped cream frosting. Next she shaved a block of dark chocolate with a fork, as per Aunt Beata's recipe, into thin long curls, then pressed them carefully with a spoon into the sides and around the outer rim of the top. In the very center, on top of the whipped cream frosting, she heaped a generous pile of fresh cherries and more chocolate curls.

She was extremely proud of the results. Hannah was forced to guard her masterpiece carefully the entire day, since her family proved incapable of passing it without reaching for a pinch of chocolate shavings or whipped cream.

"Let's bring it out," said Hannah. "Becki, honey, can you bring out the dessert plates and forks?"

"Sure thing! I mean, certainly Mother," answered

Becki, checking her childish enthusiasm.

Rodger and AJ sat there, mouths watering, waiting to see Viktor's reaction at the sight of the beautiful German cake made especially in his honor. Hannah and Becki disappeared into the house and the next thing the men heard was a scream.

Rodger leaped up in a heartbeat and ran into the house expecting to see someone hurt. What he found instead was almost as bad. Hannah stood there holding a decimated, half-empty cake plate, with tears running down her face. Becki stood there, also on the verge of tears, trying bravely to console her mother, and AJ, panic stricken, ran to look for Bodo.

Viktor entered the kitchen, surveyed the situation, and knew exactly what had happened.

"Uh, Dad . . . could you please come in here?" AJ asked nervously from the living room.

As Rodger entered the living room, he saw the fear on his son's face. Bodo was sleeping soundly, belly-up. His face and ears were covered with whipped cream, cherries and chocolate curls.

"Mom's gonna' kill us," said AJ, feeling guilty that he had not kept a better eye on his dog.

"Maybe so, son," said Rodger gently. "But we're gonna' have to face the music so it's best to get it over with."

As he entered the kitchen dragging the shame-faced, cream-and-cherry covered dog, AJ's face froze in fear.

Viktor, unable to restrain himself, burst into a deep, roaring belly laugh. Then, in a very gallant gesture, he snatched up a fork and plate and with great flourish, walked over to Hannah and scooped a large piece of the half-eaten cake onto the plate and took a bite. They all watched dumfounded.

"Madame," he announced after swallowing. "Zis is by far ze finest Black Forest cake I have ever tasted in all my life!" Then, looking over at Bodo, "Herr Bodo, you have very good taste! But zen, vhy not—after all—you are German!"

Hannah could do nothing but laugh and as she did, the tension broke. They all joined in and roared until tears rolled down their cheeks and their sides ached. Rodger took the platter from Hannah and, after scraping off the top layer of ruined cake, took a piece for himself. AJ did the same. Hannah, Becki and Nixie declined dessert.

When they finally said goodbye to Viktor, there was sadness in their parting. He had felt like family to Hannah, who had chatted in German with him about everything, especially about Uncle Ivo.

"Do you think we'll ever see him again?" she asked as they watched him leave.

"I don't know, honey, but I sure hope so."

CHAPTER FIVE

THE BRACELET

During the next few weeks AJ and Bodo, to Hannah's delight, had become inseparable. Bodo was completely at home. Hannah discovered that Bodo liked it when she spoke German to him.

It had started simply to give commands, to shoo him out of the way or coax him to move so she could vacuum under him. She soon noticed, however, that every time she spoke German, Bodo would wander over and nuzzle her hand for attention. So Hannah now spoke German freely to Bodo all day and found great comfort in it.

AJ and Rodger had started their Schutzhund training and together they went down to the beach in the cool evenings to practice. Bodo wore the leather harness, which they learned was used for tracking. Rodger appeared to be enjoying the classes as much as AJ. Bodo, just as Viktor had suspected, was already well schooled. He was the star of the class and was very patient with his new masters who didn't always know quite what to do. AJ returned after the third class with exciting news. Mr. Hartmann, the instructor, had determined that Bodo was far beyond novice and discussed with Rodger and AJ the possibility of moving him along more quickly.

He would have liked to trial Bodo immediately for his Schutzhund 1 title, but realized that neither AJ nor Rodger were skilled enough to handle him. He also knew that before a dog can be considered for Schutzhund trials, it must first receive a BH Degree.

The BH is a degree that tests a dog's temperament. The test covers basic obedience, as well as practical tests to measure the dog's reaction to everyday situations and distractions such as crowds of people, joggers, strange noises, traffic, sirens and other dogs.

Bodo had passed easily, earning his first title. AJ was so proud he would introduce him to strangers as Bodo Von Bremik BH.

As the school year rapidly wound down and the children looked forward to summer, Becki and her best friend Pam decided to get a jump on their summer tans. After changing into bathing suits, they grabbed a stack of magazines and a radio and headed out to the back yard.

"You girls want some lemonade?" Hannah shouted from the kitchen through the open window.

"Sure Mom, thanks," answered Becki.

Then resuming her conversation with Pam she continued, "Honestly, I just don't know what's wrong with that Jeremy. I mean, he acts like he likes me but he just won't ask me out."

"Maybe he's playing hard to get," offered Pam.

"Oh, look," said Becki. "We're losing the sun. We'd better move away from the trees."

As they packed up the lounge chairs, beach towels, radio and magazines, AJ brought out the lemonade tray. Hannah was surprised when he offered, but then she realized, smiling inwardly, that Pam was a very cute girl, and she was wearing a bikini.

Pam thanked AJ sweetly. Becki eyed her brother suspiciously, wondering why he always seemed to appear whenever Pam was around.

As he went back in, AJ was trying to come up with some excuse to hang around the girls. *I know—I'll train Bodo! That won't look too obvious.* So he and Bodo headed out front and began to review some training commands. AJ was very proud of his newfound handling skills and was showing off just a little, hoping to impress the girls.

Becki, still eyeing her brother suspiciously, suddenly sat up with a concerned look, grabbing her bare wrist. "My bracelet!" she shrieked. "It's gone!"

Pam sat up and together they tried to remember where she had seen it last. The bracelet, a sweet sixteen gift from her parents, was a 14kt.-gold-charm bracelet with a tiny charm the shape of a heart and she treasured it dearly.

Becki specifically remembered noticing it before they moved the chairs, so it must have fallen somewhere between the two places they'd been. They stepped very lightly so as not to bury it deeper in the sandy soil with their feet. As they continued searching through the tall, unmowed grass, Becki fought back tears. Heartbroken, she looked up at AJ, her eyes pleading for help with the search. As AJ got down on hands and knees to join the search, an idea came to him.

"Wait here," he said, as he ran off. He quickly returned with Bodo wearing his tracking harness attached to a ten-meter lead.

"This is exactly what we've been practicing in my Schutzhund class! I bet Bodo can find your bracelet!"

"Oh AJ, do you really think so?" asked Becki, hopefully.

"Uh, sure. Sure he can." said AJ, hoping he wasn't making a total fool of himself in front of Pam. As the girls watched, AJ, now pumped full of manly importance, asked for something with Becki's scent on it for Bodo to sniff.

"Here," Becki said, grabbing her beach towel off the lounge chair.

AJ placed the towel in front of Bodo. The dog sniffed it from top to bottom. Then, in a firm voice, AJ gave the command "Such!" and Bodo placed his nose to the ground. He scoured the area rapidly, his nostrils flaring wide with each sniff as he searched for a trail.

The girls had moved the chairs only a few minutes before so the scent trail was fresh and Bodo locked on to it immediately.

As Bodo followed the trail, AJ followed, being careful to give Bodo enough slack to move where he needed to go. As they moved along, AJ started to believe his plan could really work!

Bodo seemed to know what he was doing. The girls watched intently, Becki holding her breath. Finally, Bodo stopped, gave a few powerful sniffs, turned and laid down.

"That's just great!" cried Becki. "He's taking a nap!"

"No, no he's not!" AJ said, excitedly. "He's *indicating!*"

"He's what?"

"Indicating. It means he's telling me he found something! Whenever he finds an item, he lays down with it between his front paws. It's part of his Schutzhund training. Uncle Ivo taught it to him," said AJ while darting toward Bodo and dropping to his knees. He carefully ran his fingers through the tall grass until he felt something. AJ's heart leapt as he slowly lifted the bracelet out of the sandy grass. The girls were ecstatic. Becki ran over, grabbed the bracelet and gave first AJ, then Bodo, a giant, tearful hug. Pam ran over and gave AJ a quick hug and a kiss on the cheek. The kiss left AJ dazed and delighted.

"Well," he said in what Pam thought was a much deeper voice then he usually had. "If you need anything else, just call me."

AJ went back in the house and straight to the refrigerator to get Bodo a treat for a job well done. Ever since his father had been laid off, the refrigerator has seemed far less full. There was no lunchmeat or cheese. He turned to the cupboard where he found a can of squirt cheese. He took it out and looked around to make sure no one was watching. With the coast clear, he squirted a long cheese noodle into his hand and let Bodo lick it.

"Good boy," he said. "Very good boy." Bodo enjoyed

his treat so AJ repeated it a few more times. As he placed the can back in the cupboard, he saw Becki heading to her room.

"Are you guys done tanning?" he asked.

"No," she said, "I'm just putting my bracelet away for safekeeping. AJ, thank you *soooo* much for finding it!"

"Aww, you're welcome, Becks," he said as he walked back to his room.

AJ removed the tracking harness from Bodo and flopped onto his bed. Bodo spread out on the floor, still licking his nose for every morsel of cheese. AJ's mind was reeling. Lying there, hands locked behind his head, re-living his glorious moment in his imagination, he suddenly bolted upright as he realized what had just happened.

His dog had just found gold! Gold, thought AJ, I'm gonna' be rich! His mind soon filled with images of gold doubloons, pirate treasures and lost jewels. He saw himself and Bodo scouring every beach in Florida hunting for treasure, just like people did with their metal detectors.

The more he thought about it, he began to wonder why all those treasure hunters with metal detectors didn't simply use dogs. Maybe dogs can't smell gold, he wondered, but Bodo had done it. He had seen it with his own two eyes, or was this just a fluke? Could he do it again? There was only one way to find out.

Remembering what his trainer had taught him about imprinting your dog with the scent you want him to find, he slipped down the hall to Becki's room, headed over to her jewelry box and borrowed her bracelet. Now, I'll need a treat for a reward, he thought, and he headed back to the kitchen. As he opened the cupboard, Bodo, who had followed him, whined, clearly wanting more cheese.

"OK, boy, cheese it is," AJ said, as he grabbed the squirt can and went back to his room.

AJ knelt down in front of Bodo and held the bracelet for him to sniff. Then he let Bodo watch as he placed the bracelet on the floor. He started to think which German command he should use. He decided that since this was his idea, it would be in his own language.

"Bodo," he said, "find the gold!" pointing to the bracelet on the floor. Bodo walked over to the bracelet and indicated by laying down with the bracelet between his paws. AJ quickly rewarded him with a squirt of cheese, which Bodo licked eagerly.

Next, with Bodo watching, AJ placed the bracelet under a styrofoam cup with air holes punched in it and gave the command. Bodo indicated again by laying down carefully with the cup between his paws.

AJ was encouraged. His next move would be hidden

from Bodo's view. AJ added two more cups to the line-up and hid the bracelet under one of them. Bodo had no difficulty finding the bracelet. Every time Bodo found the bracelet, he was rewarded with a cheese noodle.

AJ made it more and more difficult. He began putting nickels, quarters, even pull-tabs from the kitchen trashcan under the styrofoam cups.

Each time Bodo sniffed the cups and lay down with the correct one between his paws. AJ was so happy he no longer squirted the cheese into his hand, he just squirted it right at Bodo who did his best to catch it midair.

By the time they were finished the can was empty, Bodo had crusted cheese on his forehead, and AJ was ready to go to the next level with this training. He would have to keep the bracelet for a few more hours so he hoped Becki wouldn't notice it was missing.

"No, Bodo," said AJ as he counted his change. "I need to go to the store and get more cheese." He decided the canned cheese would be the perfect treat, since it would stay in his pocket for hours without melting. Bodo whined as AJ left without him.

As AJ rode home he began to plan his strategy. He would wait until after dinner when the beach was less crowded. He would bring Bodo to an isolated part of the beach and begin his next phase of training. AJ had purchased two cans of cheese, one to replace the one he used and one for his beach excursion that night.

He paced around the house impatiently waiting for dinner time, which seemed to take forever. His chore that night was to clear the table.

He was grabbing everyone's plate before they had even finished eating when Rodger suspiciously asked, "Take it easy son, what's the big hurry tonight?"

"Oh, nothing special, I just wanna' catch the sunset, that's all."

"Oh," said Rodger, not buying it for a minute, "I see. With a can of cheese in your pants pocket?" He could see the bright yellow plastic cap sticking out of AJ's pocket.

"Oh that," AJ said. "Well . . . um . . . it's for Bodo. He loves it." Rodger just shook his head and smiled.

With his chores finished, AJ was gone in a flash to the garage for his skateboard. He and Bodo began their trip to the beach, a trip they had made many times before, but this one would be very different.

As they arrived at the beach, AJ picked up his skateboard and carried it while leading Bodo to a hidden cove on the south side. He chose a remote spot, then carefully unbuttoned his shirt pocket, removed the bracelet and placed it gently on the sand with Bodo watching.

"Find the gold!" he commanded. Bodo bent down, sniffed the bracelet and lay down with it between his paws.

"Good boy!" AJ said as he reached for his can of cheese. He continued to repeat the process, but each time, he sprinkled a fine layer of sand over the bracelet. He did it over and over, adding more and more sand. Next, he began to move Bodo further back to make him work harder to find it. Bodo was having no problem with any of this training and after each success, he was rewarded with a noodle of cheese.

Finally, AJ decided it was time for a much harder test. He tied Bodo to a tree and moved to a spot Bodo could not see. He placed the bracelet under a fine layer of sand and was extremely careful to mark its location with a few pebbles. AJ then attached his 10-meter lead to Bodo's tracking harness and firmly gave the command, "Find the gold!"

AJ's heart raced as Bodo headed in the right direction. He had his wet nose so close to the sand that as he exhaled, sand blew up, clinging to his face. Bodo ignored it, just as Ivo had trained him to do, and stayed focused on his task.

AJ was, of course, no Ivo Bremik when it came to

training dogs and his method was primitive at best, but Bodo was no ordinary dog. He represented the pinnacle of many decades of careful, selective breeding and this fact, along with the three solid years of intensive training he had received from perhaps the finest trainer in all of Europe, had prepared him for just about anything.

Bodo knew instinctively what AJ was asking him to do, and do it he did.

In less than two minutes Bodo turned and lay down. AJ's heart was now pounding, knowing Bodo was very close to the spot where he left the bracelet. He knelt down and carefully ran his fingers through the soft sand between the dogs big front paws. He felt something. He held his breath as he pulled the item from the sand.

"Yeessss!" he shouted as he grabbed the bracelet, fists clenched high in victory! Bodo jumped and ran circles around his happy young master. He was excited because he pleased AJ, which was all he really cared about.

AJ took out the cheese and danced around Bodo squirting it all over the joyful dog's face! Then he squirted it into the air, on Bodo and over his own head as he danced around, with Bodo trying to lick it off.

Then they both fell to the ground and wrestled until AJ was exhausted. Finally, they got up, covered in cheese and sand. AJ took Bodo to the water for a quick swim to clean him off. AJ tried to stay somewhat dry, but Bodo did his best to drag him playfully into the Gulf. AJ didn't resist too much, just enough so that if his parents yelled at him for swimming in his clothes he could blame the dog.

Gulfside Beach, like all of the West Coast of central Florida, is home to some of the most spectacular sunsets imaginable. Tonight was no different. As the sun set low behind AJ and Bodo, the intense red and yellow streaks filling the sky made Bodo's beautiful red coat light up even more.

As AJ left the water and turned toward home, he thought back to what Viktor had tried to tell him: Bodo was more dog than he could ever imagine.

How right you are, Mr. Adler, he thought. AJ was beginning to understand what Viktor had meant.

Upon arriving home, AJ snuck quietly into the garage and grabbed an old towel to dry Bodo. He crept to his room to change out of his wet clothes. After returning the bracelet to Becki's room, he and Bodo settled into the living room to watch television. AJ popped a bag of microwave popcorn and tossed some into the air, one at a time for Bodo to catch. Tonight he tossed him more than usual. *You earned it, Boy*, he thought. AJ wanted to tell everyone what had happened tonight, but he thought it best to wait until he was certain. After all, whether or not Bodo could actually find gold that was not planted by AJ was still a mystery. Could he make the transition to items that were lost by strangers, AJ wondered? Or was it just the scent of his family members that made it work?

With all these questions swimming around in his head, he curled up next to Bodo in the big beanbag bed and fell asleep. The cuckoo clock began to chime but Bodo just lay there, his head resting on AJ. He was now completely content.

CHAPTER SIX

BONDING

At the sound of AJ's bike tires on the gravel, Bodo was instantly at the door.

"C'mon boy," said AJ as he raced to get out of his school clothes. "I'll be right out, Tommy," he yelled to his friend who was waiting outside. AJ had decided not to tell anyone, even Tommy, about his plan to train Bodo to find gold. He still needed to work with Bodo to see if it was actually possible.

AJ was learning about tracking techniques in his Schutzhund class. He knew it would take patience and time. His plan was to train Bodo in the evening when the beaches were deserted. Since his parents would not let him go to the beach on a school night, he decided to begin serious training as soon as school ended in two weeks. Until then he would pay careful attention to everything his instructor taught him about tracking and he would ask a lot of questions. He didn't want to make any mistakes.

"Where are you boys going?" asked Hannah.

"To the park."

"Well, be sure to be home in time for dinner."

"I will, Mom."

"And don't forget Bodo's leash this time—I don't want another warning from Officer Dempsky!"

AJ ran out the door, leash in hand, Bodo following. He and Tommy disappeared around the corner on their skateboards, Bodo lopping alongside. As they began their usual race toward the park, AJ spotted the police car and yelled to his friend, "Hold up, Tommy."

"No, way!" shouted Tommy, "I'm winning!"

"But I have to stop!"

"Why?"

"I can't get caught again with Bodo off his leash, my mom will kill me!"

"Then you forfeit!" yelled Tommy as he took the lead.

AJ stopped, whipped the leash out of his pocket and quickly clipped it to Bodo.

"C'mon Bodo," he said, "let's catch him!" As he began to push off, so did Bodo, at a full gallop. AJ hung on to the leash with both hands and was about to yell, "*nein,*" but quickly regained his balance and realized what was happening. Bodo was pulling him along at an incredible speed! AJ remembered the word his mother used to tell

Bodo to move so she could vacuum under him. He tried it, "*Geh weg!*" he shouted, as he felt the air rushing past his body. "Geh weg!" he yelled again as he was rapidly closing the gap between himself and Tommy. In a few thrilling seconds he swept triumphantly past Tommy, who spun his head around in astonishment, then jumped off his skateboard to turn and stare.

"Steh!" yelled AJ, and Bodo came to a stop.

"Wow," said Tommy, catching up to his friend, "That was awesome! How'd you teach him that?"

"I don't know—he—he just did it!"

"Would he do it again?"

"I don't know, let's see!"

AJ got set up again and gave the command. Off they went, with Tommy trying unsuccessfully to keep up.

"Let me try!" cried Tommy, finally catching up and grabbing for Bodo's leash.

"Sure," said AJ.

Tommy braced himself for the jolt of the start and yelled the command he heard AJ say. "Geh weg!" but nothing happened. "Geh weg!" he repeated. Still nothing. Bodo just stood there looking at AJ.

"You must be saying it wrong," said AJ. "Bodo, Geh weg!" Bodo took off with Tommy holding on tightly.

"How do you stop him?" he yelled as he trailed away

at an exhilarating speed.

"Just hang on!" yelled AJ through cupped hands. "I'll call him back!"

Standing there watching Bodo and Tommy racing wildly away, AJ had a realization. Was it possible that Bodo would only respond to him? As he stood watching them running down the street, Viktor's words came back to him. *"Remember, a dog like zis carries a great amount of responsibility."*

He thought he understood for the first time what Viktor had tried to explain to him. Bodo was accepting him as his master, trusting him, obeying him. He also realized that Bodo would probably run until he dropped, if that's what he asked him to do.

I'm just a kid. What if I make mistakes, maybe even cause Bodo to get hurt. He's trusting me—counting on me. The weight of the responsibility frightened him. He resolved right then and there he would do his absolute best to never let anything bad happen to Bodo. He would protect him with his very life—just as he was beginning to understand Bodo would do for him. "Bodo, halt!" he yelled. "Komm boy!"

Throughout Gulfside Beach that summer, the sight of the boy on the skateboard being whisked around by the big trotting dog in the handsome leather harness was the talk in every barbershop, grocery store and gas station they zoomed past. People would smile and wave as AJ and Bodo passed by, shaking their heads and happily clearing a path for them.

Becki had been hounding her mother all afternoon.

"Mother, *pleeeeze* can I go?"

"We'll have to check with your father tonight," said Hannah for the fifth time.

"But it's not fair. Pam's mother lets her date and she's two month's younger than I am!"

"I am not Pam's mother and I said we'll see."

That night after dinner Hannah brought the subject up to Rodger.

"What do you think, hon, do we know anything about the boy?" he asked.

"He seems very sweet to me but . . ."

"Honey, you know, she is sixteen years old. We're going to have to accept that eventually. We can't just keep her locked up in her room."

"I know," said Hannah. "But the way things are today,

I just worry."

"Look," said Rodger, "if it will make you feel better, let's invite the boy over. We'll have his entire family to dinner, every single relative, then we can decide if he's good enough to roller skate with our little princess."

Hannah laughed, "OK, I get it, so I'm being a little over-protective, but . . ."

"A *little?*"

Jeremy Hanson arrived on time. He was extremely shy, well-mannered and had wonderful dimples when he smiled, which was all the time when Becki was around. He was the perfect first date for Becki. He was so nervous his hands shook as he accepted the root beer Rodger handed him.

"So," Rodger said, playing the protective father. "What time will you be bringing my daughter home?"

"Well, sir," said Jeremy, his voice cracking. "Is ten-thirty OK?"

Rodger pretended to ponder. He had actually been ready to allow her to stay out as late as eleven. "Well," he said seriously. "I think that will be fine. Is that OK with you, hon?"

"Yes," said Hannah. "Just be very careful driving."

"I will, Ma'am," said Jeremy.

To Hannah, the night seemed to drag on forever. As ten-thirty approached, she paced nervously, repeatedly looking out the window.

"Honey relax. She's gonna' think you don't trust her if you keep looking out that window!"

"I know you're right, but I just don't know what to do with myself."

"Why don't you go for a walk? Better yet, let's go sit with Benny, he's out on his porch."

"Great idea. Let's go."

"Anything to get you through this," sighed Rodger, getting out of his chair and heading out the door.

As the car pulled up at ten-thirty sharp, Hannah was relieved. She saw the two get out of the car and watched as Jeremy walked Becki to the door. But Hannah wasn't the only one watching.

From inside the house, glued to a window, Bodo saw them too. He watched as they sat down together on the front porch swing. After they had been sitting there for a few minutes talking, Jeremy shyly reached over to put his arm around Becki. Upon seeing that, Bodo turned from the window and ran to the back door. In one powerful swipe of his massive paw he slashed the screen out of the door and climbed out. He slunk soundlessly around the house and emerged on the side porch railing behind the swing. He quietly put his front paws up on the railing, his head hovering just behind Becki, who was too distracted to know he was there.

Just as Jeremy leaned over nervously, eyes closed, to kiss Becki goodnight, he felt a strange sensation of hot puffs of air on his arm. He opened his eyes to find himself face-to-face with the big dog. Bodo glared at Jeremy, his lips slightly pulled back, exposing his bright white canines. Jeremy bolted off the swing in fright, stumbled backwards and flipped completely over the railing behind him, landing on top of a low thick bush.

"Jeremy, are you all right?" screamed Becki, running down the steps to help him up. "What happened?"

"The dog," he said pointing to Bodo with a trembling hand. "He was going to attack me!"

Becki turned and saw Bodo still standing there, resting his head innocently on his front paws.

"Jeremy," she said, "it's just Bodo. He's as harmless as a pussycat!"

Jeremy got up off the ground and brushed himself off, eyes glued to the dog.

"C'mon," she said, "I promise you he's harmless, now come back and sit down."

Jeremy walked slowly around to the front of the porch to start back up the steps. Just as he lifted his foot to place it on the step, Bodo raced from the side of the porch and stood looking at him with his lips pulled back ever so slightly, just enough to flash those teeth.

"See," he said, pulling his foot back. "Look, he's growling at me!"

Becki turned to look at Bodo again, who quickly dropped his lips and smiled sweetly at her, wagging his tail in big circles.

"Jeremy, he is *not* growling at you. Look at him, he's as sweet as could be."

The instant Becki turned away, Bodo drew back his lips again at Jeremy, who was getting the message very clearly.

"Actually, I think I'd better get going. Goodnight Becki," he said backing away slowly, eyes on the protective dog. "I had a great time," he called out as he turned to run as fast as he could to his car, climbed in, locked the doors and drove quickly away.

"Well, goodnight," she called after him, confused.

"C'mon, Bodo, let's go in," she sighed. "I guess I'll just never understand men."

As she held the door for him, Bodo started through, then paused for an instant and turned his head around to scan once more for the intruder, the tiniest twitch visible on his upper lip. Satisfied, he turned happily toward Becki and trotted his way in the door, tail wagging, his eyes full of love.

"Well," said Hannah to Rodger, having witnessed the entire thing, "You were right. She is ready for dating. As long as she always takes Bodo along."

Summer break starts in mid May for the children of Gulfside Beach. With only one week of school left, excitement filled the air. Becki would finish the year on the Dean's list as expected and AJ's grades had improved as well. Nixie's elementary school had let out a week sooner than the upper grades and she was enjoying a full week of having Bodo all to herself.

Nixie adored Bodo, and he watched her far more attentively than any nanny could.

One day, as a pot of noodles boiled over in the kitchen, the jangling lid making a loud ruckus, Nixie leaped up and ran to see what the clattering sound was. Bodo bounded ahead of her and stood like a rock blocking the door to the kitchen and barking to alert Hannah. Nixie pushed and pounded him with her tiny fists, shouting all the German commands she heard Hannah use, but to no avail. The big dog just stood his ground calmly ignoring her pounding fists until Hannah arrived to take charge of the situation. "Good boy, Bodo," she said to him afterwards, marveling at how he sensed the danger and knew the difference between a child and an adult. Nixie could shout all the commands she wanted and Bodo would pick and choose which ones to obey.

On the third day of Nixie's summer vacation, she decided to play dress-up. "C'mon Bodo," she ordered, sneaking into Hannah's closet. "Let's find something for you to wear." She pulled out one of Hannah's favorite sweaters, a big, yellow, cable-knit. Next she reached for a wrap-around, floral print skirt and a floppy brimmed, straw sun hat with wide scarf-style ties.

After she finished dressing the reluctant but patient dog, she stepped back to examine her work. "Hmmm," she said, imitating Hannah when she gets dressed up. "Something's missing. I know!" and she ran to Hannah's jewelry box. She pulled out a pair of big clip-on earrings and clipped them onto Bodo's ears. Finally she added a pair of Hannah's sunglasses. She then removed her own tennis shoes and tied them onto the patient dog's front feet. "I think you look splendid, my dear," she said, promenading around Bodo.

"What are you up to, Nixie?" Hannah called from the kitchen.

"I'm just playing with Bodo," she answered. "Can I take him for a little walk?"

"Sure, but only to the corner, then come right back."

"OK, Mommy," Nixie said.

After Nixie had dressed herself, she took Hannah's mother's antique, long pearl necklace from the jewelry box and slipped it over her head. She then stepped into a pair of Hannah's high heels and grabbed a large purse.

"Come along, my dear, let's go to the mall."
Bodo hesitated, but his sense of duty compelled him to stay by her side and he reluctantly got up and walked slowly behind her, trying to shake off the tennis shoes as he walked.

Hannah's back was to them as they strolled past her and out the door.

"Come right back," Hannah yelled over her shoulder.

Nixie proudly strutted down the street with a reluctant Bodo in tow. Cars were slowing to gawk at them as they passed by.

When she reached the corner she turned to go back, just as a couple of teenage boys pulled up on bikes and started circling around them making fun of her. The ringleader was Kenny Bozwell, the arrogant youngest son of Clinton Bozwell. Kenny, like his notorious older brother Billy, was always in trouble. Rodger warned his children repeatedly to stay away from the Bozwell boys.

It didn't take long for Kenny to spot the valuable necklace. The bully began to follow them, while planning a way to get his hands on it. Nixie, acting very proud, marched on without so much as a backward glance.

"Look, I'm really sorry I laughed at you, so, how 'bout if you let me pet your dog?" asked the skinny, unkempt youth.

"No!" Nixie snapped.

"Aw, c'mon. I really am sorry. I think you look *real peerty.*"

"You *dooo*?" said Nixie, stopping to reconsider.

"Yeah, sure I do."

"Well, OK. Just one pet."

Kenny looked over at the ridiculous dog in the earrings, sunglasses and straw hat and perceived no threat. *Stupid mutt,* he thought as he lay his bike down and approached them. He was thinking his best plan of attack would be to pretend to reach for the dog but to grab the pearls instead.

Bodo, seeing the stranger approach Nixie, slowly moved his body between her and the youth. As the boy reached his hand out toward Nixie, the sound of Bodo's growl was so sudden and so loud he could feel the vibration of it running through him. At the same instant, the sunglasses rose up on the dogs face as he curled his lips back and bared his teeth in warning. Nixie stood there terrified, having never seen Bodo growl before. The youth froze, his hand still outstretched in mid-air.

What the boy could not have known, was that Bodo, like all boxers, had a very protective nature, especially toward children. Bodo would never have allowed a threatening hand to touch his charge. Bodo would have protected Nixie with his last breath.

"C'mon," yelled another boy. "What's taking so long? Hurry up, will ya?"

The boy made one small move closer to Nixie to test the dog. Bodo's growl got extremely severe. The boy stood paralyzed, his hand still outstretched toward Nixie, afraid to move in any direction.

That is the scene AJ saw as he rounded the corner. AJ, recognizing instantly the protective stand Bodo had assumed and hearing the low rumbling growl, yelled "nien!" and Bodo relaxed. The youth slowly retracted his arm, took two steps backward and fell over his bike. Bodo walked toward the bike, lifted his leg, skirt and all, and did his business on the back tire.

The boy, afraid to move with the dog so near, lay

frozen until Bodo finished and then turned away with his head and tail held high in triumph. The boy scrambled up, jumped on the bike and sped off toward his friends.

"What happened, Nixie? Are you all right?"

Nixie looked up at her big brother with tears rolling down her cheeks. She didn't understand what had taken place. "I was just taking Bodo for a walk," she sobbed. "And that boy was bad. He was laughing at us and . . ."

AJ put his arms around her. "Awww, don't cry, Nixie, please don't cry." As he hugged her to stop the tears, he looked over at Bodo in skirt, hat and sunglasses, thinking how ridiculous he looked.

He wanted to scold Nixie but could not. "Well, I think you look really nice, Nixie," he said, standing back to admire her outfit, his eyes falling on the necklace. He remembered the outstretched hand frozen in the air. *Grandmom's pearls!*

"The pearls, Nixie!" he shouted at her, "Grandmom's pearls. They were trying to steal the pearls!"

"Oh, AJ, I'm *sorry*," cried Nixie, "Mommy's gonna' be really mad."

"Don't worry Nixie, we'll put everything back like it was and she won't ever know, OK?"

"OK," Nixie said sobbing. AJ took off his backpack and emptied out the books. He removed the sweater and skirt from a grateful Bodo and stuffed them into the empty bag, along with the pearls, high heels, dress and scarf Nixie had been wearing and put his books under his arm.

"Hurry, put on your shoes. You're gonna' have to wear the hat, it won't fit in my backpack and carry this," he said, as he picked up the big pocketbook she had dropped on the sidewalk during the commotion.

"Hurry, before Mom looks for you."

Smiling at last, Nixie quickly put on her shoes, hat and sunglasses and picked up the pocketbook.

"OK, ladies," AJ said with a note of sarcasm toward Bodo, taking Nixie's hand. "Shall we go home?"

Nixie walked proudly toward home, holding AJ's hand, content in the knowledge that she had the best big brother in the whole world and that he and Bodo would never let anything bad happen to her.

As they scurried quickly through the kitchen, Hannah, leaning over the stove, heard them come in and glanced over her shoulder. Thinking she had seen something strange, she looked back but they were gone. That's odd, she thought, shaking her head. No, it couldn't be. I must be imagining things. I could have sworn I just saw Bodo walk by wearing earrings.

CHAPTER SEVEN

School's Out!

With school finally out for the summer, AJ was now free to focus all his attention on Bodo. He had been working with Bodo using Becki's bracelet whenever he could and he felt the time had come to test Bodo's tracking skills without it.

With dinner and dishes completed, AJ geared up, placed the tracking harness on Bodo and pointed him toward the beach. Off they went in a flash.

As they hit the sand, AJ put his skateboard into his backpack, which carried water and snacks for himself and Bodo. As he removed his six-foot leash from Bodo and replaced it with the ten-meter lead, Bodo knew instinctively what he was about to be asked to do. The actual command was just a formality. AJ let out the slack on the lead and drew a breath.

"Find the gold!" he said, and they were off. Neither Bodo nor AJ had a clue as to where to look for lost jewelry. AJ had planned to start with Gulfside Beach and eventually work his way both north and south to the surrounding beach towns. When he had finished combing them all, he would just start over again.

It didn't take long for AJ to realize that this would be a lot harder than he imagined. They covered block after block of beach with no reaction from Bodo.

After forty-five minutes of walking, AJ looked up to see the familiar face of Maximillion Mumpford, the prospector.

Maximillion was a much-liked fixture around Gulfside Beach. He had a full head of long white hair which he pulled back hippy-style into a ponytail. No one really knew what he did for a living, or if, in fact, he had ever had a job. But they knew you could set your watch by his appearance at the beach with his metal detector every sunrise and sunset. He was an interesting and knowledgeable fellow who would engage any stranger in a long friendly chat as though he had known them all his life. His favorite subject was, of course, treasure hunting. His dream was to strike it rich someday by turning up some ancient coin or artifact from a long lost civilization or from a sunken pirate ship. He had a lot of schemes and theories about hunting for treasure and he had a lot of friends.

"Any luck today, Mr. Mumpford?" AJ asked.

"Na," said the prospector, straightening his back and stretching. "Just pull-tabs and bottle caps as usual."

"Have you ever found anything good?" asked AJ.

"Why sure," said Maximillion, his eyes growing wide. "Over the years I've recovered thousands of dollars worth of coins and lost jewelry from these beaches, plus lots of other cool stuff too. Here, look at this." He held out his hand to show AJ a ring made out of a spoon.

"Wow," said AJ, "that's really cool. But how do you know where to look?"

"Well," said the old hippy, "you kinda' develop a sense for it after you've been at it awhile, but I've learned a few tricks over the years."

"Really?" said AJ. "*Weeeell,*—supposin' a fellow wanted to get himself a metal detector and get started hunting for treasure. What would this fellow need to know?"

The old hippy scratched his chin in thought. "The first thing I would tell you—er—this fellow, is you gotta' work the splash zone," said Maximillion.

"Splash zone?"

"Yep. The splash zone. You see that mark on the beach from the high tide?" he said as he pointed to the high water mark.

"Yes, I see it."

"OK, you would tell this fellow that the area between the high tide mark and the water level at low tide is called the splash zone. That's the area where people run and jump and swim and throw their children into the air. All that crazy jumpin' around while they're all wet is what causes their jewelry to slip off, and that's where I look for it."

"Hmmmm, I think I get it," AJ said. "Anything else I should know—er—tell this fellow?"

"Well, some of my very best detecting is done right after storms."

"Storms?"

" Yep. Right after a storm, just as soon as the wind eases up to the point where I can stand without being blown over, I head out with my detector. The storms move the sand around on the beach covering some things and uncovering others. At the same time the churning waters kick up long-buried items from under the Gulf and some get left behind on the beach when the water recedes," said the seasoned prospector.

"Wow, that's great advice!" said AJ. "Thanks, Mr. Mumpford!"

"Any time."

AJ took his time as he walked Bodo far away. He didn't want the prospector to hear him give Bodo the "find the gold" command. After they were out of earshot, AJ headed Bodo into the splash zone, eased up on the lead and gave the command.

Bodo went right to work and the pair covered several more blocks of beach, but to no avail. AJ was becoming very discouraged. Maybe he was asking more of Bodo than he could do. As he reached the outskirts of the next town to the south, he realized he'd better turn back if he wanted to make it home before dark.

He moved Bodo away from the splash zone and they sat down on the sand to take a break. He removed his bottled water and a pack of peanut butter crackers from his backpack. He split the crackers with Bodo, then tilted his water bottle so he could let Bodo have a drink. As he sat there looking down at Bodo, who was now sitting in the sand scratching his ear, he realized that even if he spent the whole summer searching for jewelry and came up completely empty-handed, the time he spent on the beach with Bodo made it all worthwhile.

AJ stood up and prepared for the long walk back. Bodo assumed his position out in front waiting for his command.

"Find the gold," AJ told him again and off they went. This time, since they had already searched the splash zone, they moved farther back from the water line and began searching the area of the beach where the sunbathers spread out on their blankets and lounge chairs. AJ carefully guided Bodo around them. It was almost dark when they neared the small parking lot of the beach nearest his home.

He nudged Bodo on a path that would lead them straight to the parking lot and then home. It was there, only a few hundred yards from the parking lot, that Bodo suddenly altered his course. He stopped; nose fixed over the sand, gave a few big sniffs, and lay down.

AJ just stood staring, afraid to get his hopes too high. They had been searching for almost two hours. Bodo waited patiently as AJ knelt down and sifted through the soft sand. He felt something. As he lifted it from the sand he held his breath—it was a herringbone bracelet. He looked at the clasp. It read 14kt. "Good boy, Bodo! Good boy!" he shouted, still hardly believing his eyes. He had done it! He had found gold, and this time it didn't have Becki's scent on it. Bodo's tail wagged happily as he soaked up the praise and head-scratching from his master.

AJ pulled out the can of squirt cheese and danced around as he squirted a foot long cheese noodle into the air for Bodo to catch. Bodo ate up the cheese and sensing AJ's excitement, pounced playfully around him with his front paws down and his tail up. AJ responded to the invitation and wrestled Bodo down into the sand.

As they geared up for their skateboard ride home, AJ's thoughts were bursting with excitement and plans for all the gold he and Bodo would uncover in the days to come. He felt certain that his life was about to change in a very big way.

The outcome of his first search had left him thrilled, and also hooked. When he reached home, he put all his gear in the garage and went to the kitchen for a snack. All that walking had made him very hungry. He grabbed the peanut butter and spread what little was at the bottom of the jar on some bread and poured himself a glass of milk. Then he took a spoon and scraped out the last of it, and making sure no one was watching, held the spoon for Bodo. When the spoon was clean, he let Bodo lick out the plastic jar. He laughed as Bodo struggled to reach the bottom of the jar, shoving his big nose in as far as it would fit. When he was finished, he picked up the plastic jar to throw it away, but changed his mind and went to the sink to wash it out instead. It would be the perfect place to store his loot from the beach. He then dried it carefully and placed the bracelet he had found into the jar. After screwing on the lid, he went to his room to hide it in the back of his closet.

AJ lay in bed that night unable to sleep. Something was bothering him. He had been thrilled at first after finding that bracelet on the beach, but now, it was all starting to feel wrong. He couldn't help thinking of how upset Becki was when she had lost her sweet sixteen bracelet. Someone once owned that bracelet and was most likely heartbroken over losing it. He thought about what he would do with it. If he tried to sell it, who would he sell it to? He knew his family could use the money, but was it wrong to sell jewelry that rightfully belonged to someone else?

Does finding something really mean you own it and if so, does that mean he now owned Becki's bracelet since he and Bodo had found it?

Of course not, you idiot, he thought. So why is this bracelet different? Is it because he didn't know the person who lost it?

The questions were just too complicated to answer. He would need more time to figure this out. *I'll think about it later,* he promised himself. His thoughts then turned to his dog.

AJ was extremely proud of Bodo. As he added it up in his head, he figured out they had searched about three miles of beach. That's amazing, he thought, and during all that time Bodo never once let up. He had scoured those miles with his nose to the ground every step. He searched for that jewelry as intently as if he were searching for a lost child, or trailing an escaped convict. It was only jewelry, but to Bodo it was far more than that. It was a way to please his young master. That was his motivation, his driving force. The fact was Bodo would have searched that beach all night if that's what AJ had wanted. All he had to do was ask.

As early summer headed into mid-summer, AJ and Bodo combed the sands of Gulfside Beach and the surrounding areas four or five times a week. He was beginning to develop a sense of where to look for lost jewelry, just as Maximillion had said.

He soon realized that the splash zone might be good for metal detectors, but it was not good for Bodo. He never alerted one single time in the splash zone. When Bodo did alert, it always seemed to be around areas of high foot traffic. Along the paths from the parking lots to the beaches, or under the wooden stairs from the hotel pool decks that led down to the beach. The best spot was the wide-open span of beach above the high-water line, where the sunbathers lay and children would frolic with their beach toys.

AJ's peanut butter jar was starting to get heavy and valuable as the summer advanced.

One particular evening late in June, just as the sun was beginning to set, AJ and Bodo were working the northern portion of Gulfside Beach, searching along a well-used path leading from a hotel parking lot down to midbeach when Bodo alerted. AJ kneeled down to check the sand between Bodo's paws, and as usual Bodo was correct. AJ lifted a diamond-cut rope chain necklace from the sand. He checked the clasp. *Yes*, he said to himself— 14kt. He wiped off the remaining sand and slid it into his shirt pocket. Just then, he was startled by a familiar voice.

"Now that's something you don't see every day."

AJ spun around to see Maximillion Mumpford standing behind him.

"A dog that can find gold."

AJ began to panic.

After taking a moment to absorb the impact of what he had just seen, the old hippy scratched his jaw and spoke slowly. "Supposin' a fellow wanted to get himself a dog—and supposin' this fellow wanted to teach that dog to find gold. What might you say to such a fellow to get him started?"

AJ, very nervous about his secret getting out, stood up and looked Maximillion squarely in the eye and answered, "Well, the first thing I'd tell this fellow is, if he did manage, by some fluke, to teach a dog to find gold, the first thing he should do is keep it to himself."

"Why, naturally," said the sly old prospector, looking back, eye-to-eye, completely understanding AJ's meaning and agreeing with a wink and a nod. "Why, a thing like that getting out could be very bad for business."

The silent agreement now made between the two of them, AJ continued, "OK, the first thing this fellow would need to do, of course, is get a dog."

"Any special kind of dog?"

"Well, a smart one for sure. Then, this fellow would need to imprint the smell of the go—," he paused. "Of the thing he wants the dog to find," he said.

"Imprint, eh?"

"That's right," said AJ. With great detail he then told Maximillion exactly what he had done to train Bodo to find gold.

"Hmmm," said the old hippy, "This sure does give a fellow something to think about." He then thanked AJ sincerely and moved on, very deep in thought.

After leaving Maximillion, AJ continued working his

way north on Gulfside Beach. He was a little rattled at having Bodo's special skill uncovered, even with the silent understanding he now shared with his fellow prospector.

As the month of June came to a close and the Fourth of July was fast approaching, AJ's peanut butter jar continued to fill up.

Over the summer he and Bodo had combed endless miles of beaches, parking lots and tourist trails. He liked to go through his treasures late at night, long after everyone else had gone to sleep. AJ would pull the jar out of its secret hiding place and dump everything onto the bed. Then he would line up his treasures and, one by one, relive the thrill of each find, reminiscing about the time, place, and memories attached to each piece. But his favorite memory of all was attached to a piece of jewelry that never made it into his peanut butter jar.

On the shore of Gulfside Beach, at the northernmost end, stood a picnic pavilion with tables, benches, a water fountain and a few big blue municipal trash barrels. It's a favorite place for visitors to take a break from the heat of the Florida sun and enjoy a meal. AJ and Bodo would usually stop there for a rest, whenever they worked this beach.

There was someone AJ knew would always be there, and he looked forward to seeing him. Everyone knew him as Crabby Gus. AJ liked Crabby Gus and the old man seemed to enjoy AJ's company as well. Gus liked to fuss over Bodo, rubbing his head or scratching him behind his floppy ears.

Crabby Gus, whose real name was Gustave Olofsson, had spent his entire life as a stone crabber. He was the son of a Swedish fisherman, who was the son of a fisherman, who was the son of . . . for as far back as old Gus knew.

Crabby Gus had crabbed off an old rickety, but sea worthy, crabbing boat that had been his father's, and that also served as his home.

Stone crabbing is a risky and dangerous way to earn a living, but it was what he knew and he loved it. Stone crabs are very unique creatures. They inhabit the deep waters along the coast from North Carolina to Mexico, but are most abundant in the rich Florida waters.

They are unique because they possess the ability to throw off their powerful black-tipped claws when caught, and re-grow the claw, up to three or four times during their lifetime. For this reason, only the claws are harvested, the crabs are always thrown back. Stone crab season lasts only seven months, ending in May, so Gus would switch to fishing for grouper or shark the rest of the year.

That had been Gus' life until a few years ago. A sudden storm had hit the Gulf Coast nearly destroying the rickety old fishing vessel. It now sat in dry dock broken, battered and covered in cobwebs. The cost to restore her was so great that Gus realized he would probably never see her sea-worthy again.

Crabby Gus had not a single hair on his head but his wild gray beard grew freely. Sailor tattoos ran up and down both his thin arms. He had a large, tall frame when he managed to straighten up to his full height, which was difficult for him. It was obvious that Crabby Gus had once been a tower of a man. It was also obvious that the old mariner was homeless. AJ knew this because, in addition to the tattered clothes and unshaven face, he had seen Gus spread newspapers on one of the benches late one evening, then lay down upon them to sleep. He hadn't wanted to embarrass the old fellow so he had quietly turned around and headed the other way.

But it had haunted him. He knew how much fear he sensed in his own parents at his father's loss of his job, even though they tried to act as if everything was normal. He wondered what it must be like for the old man, with nowhere to go, no one to talk to, no bed, no pillow, no refrigerator filled with food, no clothes except what he wore on his back, no television or skateboard or dog.

AJ realized that compared to Crabby Gus, he was very blessed. Even if the refrigerator and cupboards were not overflowing with food as they had once been and even if he didn't get anything new in a very long time, he realized he had more than he could ever want. He had his family, a safe home, and now he had Bodo.

As AJ approached the pavilion on this particular night, he called to Gus, who was still way in the distance.

"Ahoy there young matey," Gus shouted back.

"How ya doin' today, Gus?" asked AJ.

"Fair to middlin', how's by you?"

"Oh, we're OK. Seen any dolphins today?"

And so they began their usual dialog about life on and around the Gulf. As they sat there in the cool breeze, making small talk, to fill the silence, AJ said, "Hey Gus, did you ever have the grouper sandwich special they serve over at the Gulfside Grill? My dad and I tried it last Saturday and it was great!"

"Why, no, young matey, can't say as I have," said Gus.

"Gee, Gus, how come? Don't you like grouper?"

No sooner had the words left his mouth, AJ was horrified as he realized his mistake, and angry with himself for being so stupid. The old man probably got most of his meals from the surrounding barrels filled with the scraps and leftovers of picnickers each day.

Then, without a second thought, AJ jumped to his feet, reached into his shirt pocket and pulled something out. He held his clenched fist in the air, motioning to the old fellow to open his hand. The old man did, expecting a handout of a few coins like the daily passer-byers would sometimes give him. He was shocked when he looked in his hand and saw a beautiful 14kt. gold charm bracelet with three tiny charms. AJ had just lifted it from the beach no more than twenty minutes ago.

The proud old man's brow was lined with worry as he tried to give it back.

"Son, I can't take this," he said, shaking his head. "I just can't."

"Sure you can," said AJ, "I've got three more at home just like it. Bodo finds—uh, I mean I always find things in the sand. I'm just lucky, I guess. Besides, it's a girl's bracelet. What am I going to do with a girl's bracelet?"

The old man looked away in embarrassment. He didn't know how to show AJ his gratitude or how to let him know how much this small treasure meant to him.

AJ broke the awkward silence. "Well, so long Gus, I gotta' get goin'," he said as he rose to leave. Then, over his shoulder he added, "And next time I see you, tell me how the sandwich was."

Then he and Bodo turned back toward town and continued their searching. When AJ looked back, old Gus was staring down into the palm of his hand and wiping his eye on his sleeve.

The next morning the old timer pawned the bracelet and got slightly over fifty dollars, enough for a few hearty meals including the grouper sandwich AJ had suggested.

He walked proudly over to the Gulfside Grill and ordered a grouper sandwich special with fries and coleslaw. The waitress, looking at the rag tag old man strangely, informed him that grouper was on the lunch menu, and it was only nine-thirty in the morning.

"Oh?" he said, guessing her thoughts. He then reached into his pocket and proudly showed off a twenty-dollar bill and said, "Well then, you'd better bring me some coffee and pie while I wait." Then smiling a big, happy grin, he said, "I have all day."

CHAPTER EIGHT

The Fourth of July

It was the morning of the Fourth of July. Rodger had been officially out of work for almost six weeks. Finding employment in a small town that has lost its biggest employer was proving impossible.

He had gone down to the fishing docks and talked to every captain of every fishing boat. Most of them knew him. Rodger had spent most of his boyhood aboard a shrimp boat. His father, a widower much too soon, had done his best to raise the boy alone, but all he knew was shrimping. Having fished the rich waters of the Gulf all his life, that was what he taught his son.

Rodger knew everything there was to know about shrimping, boats, equipment, and, of course, the Gulf.

When he was a boy, he would run home from school and scramble aboard the big shrimp boat his father owned and head straight down below deck to do his homework, while the men above deck geared up to head out.

His father harvested the nocturnal shrimp species that flourished in the Gulf of Mexico and after he finished his homework he was allowed to work with the men until he was so tired he couldn't stand upright.

His father would take him below and put him to bed in a little bunk and in the morning, they would go ashore to the two rooms his father rented above the local bait shop. There he would eat the breakfast his father prepared for the two of them, clean up, change his clothes and head back to school. Rodger thought it was the most perfect childhood a boy could have.

He had been finding occasional work on the shrimp boats whenever they found themselves shorthanded. He loved being on the water again, but the idea of not being home at night was hard to get used to.

Hannah had been trying to get more hours at the nursing home, but with so many townspeople in the same predicament, the hours were not available. Six weeks without a paycheck made money tight.

Each week they had been tapping into what little savings they had just to buy groceries. Hannah was delighted to have a holiday to spend with the kids. Things had been very tense in their home lately and she worried about Rodger. He was not dealing with unemployment very well. She hoped a day of old-fashioned activities and fun would improve his mood.

"Oh honey, what are you doing up? I was hoping you'd get some rest today. What time did you dock last night?" she asked, as Rodger joined AJ and Nixie at the kitchen table.

"I got plenty of sleep," said Rodger, who could not get used to the idea of sleeping during the day. "We wrapped up a little earlier then usual." Rodger was glad the captain of the *Aquarius* had called him to fill in for a few days for one of the guys whose wife was expecting a baby any day. The man didn't want to be miles out in the Gulf when the baby came.

"How about some eggs?" Hannah asked.

"Sounds good," said Rodger. "Do we have any bacon to go with them?"

"You're in luck," said Hannah, handing him a mug of coffee.

"Scrambled or fried?"

"Scrambled would be great. Thanks, hon."

"Daddy," said Nixie, "after the parade, I'm gonna' get a butterfly on my face!"

"That's nice," said Rodger, only half listening, as he opened the morning paper to scan the want ads.

"Oh, that reminds me, hon, could you pull out the section on the activities scheduled for today? I want to see what time they're doing the children's face painting," asked Hannah.

"Are you guys planning to enter any of the father-son races?" Hannah asked AJ and Rodger.

"Well, I don't know," said Rodger, flipping through the paper. "What do you think Son? Do you want to enter a potato sack race with your old man?"

"Gee Dad, I'm kinda' old for that stuff," said AJ, as he sneaked some of his scrambled eggs under the table to Bodo. Then, hearing a knock at the door, he looked up to see who it was.

"Hi, Pam," said Hannah, opening the door. "C'mon in. Would you like some breakfast?"

"Oh, no thank you, Mrs. Jenkins. Is Becki up yet?"

"She's trying out a new hair-style. You can go on back," said Hannah. "And tell her to get out here soon if she wants some breakfast."

"OK. Hi AJ," said Pam, waving to him as she flitted by. Ever since the bracelet incident, Pam had developed a new respect for her best friend's little brother.

"Hi, Pam," said AJ, using his much deeper manly voice. Rodger glanced at Hannah and they hid their amusement artfully.

"So, what are your plans for the day, AJ?" Hannah asked her son. She had been increasingly concerned about him lately. He seemed to do nothing but walk the beaches with Bodo, day after day. Whenever she asked him about his walks, he just answered that he and Bodo were training. In fact, his weekly training classes with Bodo were about the only thing he seemed interested in.

Rodger had skipped the last few classes because he was filling in on the shrimp boats. He missed the time with his son, but he knew Bodo was much more comfortable with AJ than with his own awkward attempts to learn the techniques, and he was secretly relieved to get out of going.

Hannah was hoping AJ would participate in some of the activities planned for the young people. But it wasn't the Fourth of July that interested AJ, it was the fifth.

He did have plans to go to the daylong celebration, but it was not to play games. AJ was planning to scout out the spots where the activities were being held, so he would know exactly where to search the next day. With events like foot races, volleyball, informal football games and tens of thousands of locals and tourists frolicking on the beach and swimming in the Gulf, the odds were good a few people would lose jewelry.

"Oh, I was just gonna' go down to the beach with Tommy to check out what's happening," AJ said.

"Wonderful, are you boys planning to compete in

anything? I hear there's big prizes for frisbee and volleyball this year."

"Aw, Mom, you know I'm not very good at those things. But Tommy wants to try the water guns."

"Well, have fun. Just be sure to be careful, and don't stay in the hot sun too long," said Hannah, delighted that AJ was planning to do something besides work with Bodo.

As AJ got up from the table and put his dish in the sink, Bodo became eager, thinking he was going. AJ looked his dog straight in the eye. "Not this time boy, you're staying here. Too much traffic out there today for you." The big dog, who had been panting in anticipation, suddenly retracted his tongue, and closed his mouth in silence. The wrinkles on his face deepened as he studied the situation. Bodo was not pleased as AJ rode off on his bike without him, but the mood would pass quickly.

Bodo, like all boxers, had an enthusiastic love of life and family, so he quickly turned from the door and looked around for Hannah, deciding he would help her do her chores. As Hannah loaded the dishwasher with the breakfast dishes, Bodo proceeded to lick clean those he could reach. It was his favorite job.

The town center was abuzz with excitement as the preparations got under way. The State Champion high school marching band was gearing up for the parade, and almost every bike in town was covered with crepe paper and flags. The parade would start on the green in the center of town and end at the beach, where big tents were already being hoisted up to shade the food vendors and picnic tables. A spectacular fireworks display over the water in the evening would complete the Fourth of July festivities. It was a typical small American town, like so many others, the only difference being that this town had a beach.

Tommy and AJ sat on their bikes watching the parade. The marching band passed by playing *Stars and Stripes Forever*. The mayor of the town followed the band in a classic Chevrolet convertible with the top down. The car was decked out in streamers and flags, with a cardboard sign attached to the front that read "Mayor Waylon Pennywell." The ponderous old mayor smiled and waved as he passed, sweating profusely, though the day was only beginning to heat up.

The two boys spent the day at several local beaches. They hung around watching the girls play volleyball, eating pizza and snow cones and trying their hand at some of the games.

AJ, much to his astonishment, won a large stuffed animal by tossing a softball into an old-fashioned metal milk jug. It was a purple hippo with an Uncle Sam hat on its head. He was hoping for the baseball bat and glove.

He was very proud when he won but was mortified when the man running the booth handed him his prize. He quickly stuffed it into a black trash bag he scavenged from a nearby trash barrel to hide it and tied it to the back of his bike. He planned to give it to Nixie, but saw no sense in being seen with it. He was about to set off on his bike to the last spot he had seen Hannah and Nixie, in line for the children's pie-eating contest.

He was very anxious to receive the proud accolades from his mother and to relieve himself of the ridiculous stuffed animal. Tommy had gone ahead to the ice cream stand and they were to meet there after he got rid of the hippo. As he finished securing the bag to his bike, he was startled by a voice behind him. "What'cha got in the bag, punk?" said the deep threatening voice. AJ turned around to see the towering figure of Billy Bozwell, Kenny's older brother. He was leaning on a tent pole, smirking and spitting peanut shells toward AJ.

"Nothing that concerns you!" said AJ in a falsely confident voice. Bozzy, as he was called, was a moose in size, standing well over six-feet tall and weighing two-hundred-eighty pounds. He terrorized the town on his flashy Suzuki Street Extreme Sportbike, wearing a black leather biker's jacket no matter how hot the temperature.

Bozzy was trouble. AJ knew it. The police knew it. Everyone in town knew it. He was an arrogant juvenile offender with a mile-long record, who's influential father always managed to pull the necessary strings whenever he got in trouble. He was, in his own mind, invincible—far above the law and free to do whatever he pleased.

"Yeah, well why don't I just see for myself, smart mouth," he said as he stepped forward, throwing the empty peanut bag on the ground and grabbing the handlebars of AJ's bike. AJ tried to pull away, but Bozzy held him fast. "Let me go!" demanded AJ.

"Or what?" sneered Bozzy. "You'll tell your mommy?" AJ continued to struggle to pull free, but Bozzy just held him there laughing. "So let's see what you're hiding," he said as he yanked the black bag off AJ's bike with one hand, the other still holding him captive. Then he pulled out the stuffed animal. "Well, looky here, we got us a perty little purple hippopotamus!" He already knew what was in the bag. He had watched with jealous rage as AJ tossed the softball into the milk can and won, after he had spent more than twenty dollars trying. He had promised his girlfriend a hippo.

"No sweat, Baby," he told her, "any idiot can do it." But he couldn't. Convinced that the game was rigged, he angrily demanded his money back, but the tough, burly man running the game had just laughed at him.

He was burning with shame and humiliation, and was planning to steal one when the man's back was turned, just as AJ came along and plunked the two dollars down for three balls and sunk one on the second try.

"Put that down, you jerk!" yelled AJ, angrily, trying to pull it out of the thug's hand. "It's for my little sister, you give it back!"

"I'll bet you don't even have a little sister. In fact, I'll bet this is for you! A fuzzy stuffed animal to sleep with, ain't that right?" Bozzy jeered.

AJ was furious. People began to gather around to watch, but no one dared stand up to Billy Bozwell.

"In fact, you probably stole it off some little kid," he said loud enough for the onlookers to hear. "No way a scrawny punk like you could win it. You stole it didn't you!" he yelled.

AJ stood his ground bravely, but he was no match for Bozwell. As he began to protest his innocence, Bozzy kicked the bike over hard, sideways, to the ground, and still holding on to the stuffed animal, said, "That'll teach you to steal toys from little kids. Now get out'a here punk, before I teach you a real lesson!"

AJ scrambled to his feet and took off, seething with anger. When he caught up to Tommy, he was too humiliated to tell him what had happened.

"Did Nixie like it?" Tommy asked.

"Oh, ah, I guess so. C'mon, let's go someplace else."

As dusk approached, Becki and Pam headed to the area of the beach where a rock and roll band was setting up. Hannah and Rodger were settling down with Nixie in the sand to watch the fireworks and AJ and Tommy set out on their own. They had already decided to watch the fireworks over in Sabal Palms, the next town to the south of Gulfside Beach. It was a much larger town and always had the biggest and most spectacular fireworks in the area. The absolute best place to watch from was Moccasin Head Point, an isolated swath of land that projected far out into the Gulf of Mexico, accessible only on foot by way of an unmarked trail the locals called Pirate Bones Path.

The boys met up with two other friends on the way over and the four of them made their way on bikes. When they finally reached the entrance to the path, they threw their bikes behind some bushes and set out on foot.

Dusk was well upon them as they made their way along the narrow winding path, which began to take on a very sinister feel as the shadows lengthened and the darkness deepened. Carefully they snaked their way along in single file toward the tip of Moccasin Head Point. Once there, it was very clear what the old mariners meant whenever they talked about the Point.

Moccasin Head Point was intensely beautiful by day. The view was unmatched anywhere up or down the coast. At night though, it was a much different story. The thin strip of land jutting far out into the Gulf of Mexico was too small for a lighthouse, and in the darkness of night, would simply vanish. It was then that Moccasin Head Point would become as treacherous to passing boats as its namesake, the deadly poisonous Water Moccasin. AJ and his friends staked out their spots in the sand and settled back to watch a spectacular fireworks display. Within minutes, the first bright explosions lit up the night sky with pink, yellow and blue trails of fire, streaming out in wonderful starbursts that reflected brightly off the dark Gulf waters.

CHAPTER NINE

Pirate Bones Path

On the morning of the fifth of July, AJ awoke early. He ate cereal while Rodger read the want ads over his morning coffee. Hannah had already left for work. "So, what do you have planned to do today?" asked Rodger, looking over his paper.

"Nothing much. I thought I'd just hit the beach."

"Hmmm," said Rodger, "are you meeting up with Tommy?" Like Hannah, Rodger was beginning to wonder why his son spent so much time alone at the beach.

"No, just me and Bodo," he answered. Rodger just shook his head. He thought of pressing AJ for more answers but decided against it, thinking it was probably just another phase of growing up and it would pass. Perhaps he was just checking out the girls on the beach.

After loading up his backpack with snacks and water for himself and Bodo, he set out on his bike for what he hoped would be their most successful prospecting trip ever. His plan, which he had carefully mapped out the day before, was to spend the entire morning searching Sea Otter Cove. He had never searched that far north. After finishing there he would return home for lunch to escape the intense mid-day sun. After dinner he would head out in a southerly direction to search the beach at Sabal Palms, which would also be a new experience for him. He had carefully noted each spot he thought would be the ideal place to find treasure. Anywhere that had high foot traffic or activities, or where tourists had gathered, he and Bodo would search.

Sea Otter Cove is a beautiful horseshoe-shaped beach. When he surveyed it yesterday, he noticed the southern end of the beach was far more crowded—a local radio station had been doing live broadcasts from there.

He eased Bodo on a path in that general direction and gave the command, "Find the gold." It did not take long. Bodo alerted in less than five minutes. AJ retrieved a 14kt. gold ankle bracelet from that spot. Next, they rounded the area that had been used as a makeshift dance floor. AJ thought to himself with all that jumping around, surely somebody had to lose something. Once again his sense was correct. Bodo alerted near the center of the sand dance floor and AJ lifted a tiny 14kt. gold ring with a blue stone. AJ was not sure if it was a toe or finger ring, but either way it would go in his peanut butter jar when he got home. Bodo did not alert again so AJ pointed him to the north side of the cove. Yesterday someone had strung a volleyball net between two palm trees and the game had gone on all day. If someone had to leave, someone else from the crowd would fill in their spot. AJ thought that area could be productive. They searched the entire area, and Bodo did not alert once. As AJ was about to call it a morning, Bodo pulled him toward a lone Sabal palm tree. There he alerted at the base of the tree. AJ looked down and spotted a thick, man's gold chain in a tiny little pile. He picked it up and noticed it had broken midway. He reasoned someone must have broken it during the game and placed it next to the root of this tree for safekeeping. During the excitement of the game, the owner must have forgotten to retrieve it. He pocketed it and rewarded Bodo with a squirt of cheese, then said, "Well I guess that's it for this beach, boy—it's getting hot, let's head for home." They left Sea Otter Cove and journeyed toward home, eventually reaching the covered pavilion that marked the northern boundary of Gulfside Beach. As usual, they would rest here, have their snacks and water and chat with Crabby Gus.

"Ahoy there young Matey," shouted Gus, waving to AJ.

"Hi, Gus," said AJ. "Did you watch the fireworks last night?"

"Oh *yes*," said the old man, clapping his hands like a little child. "It was so beautiful, yes siree, beautiful."

"Say, did you ever get that grouper sandwich?"

"Oh, let me tell you, matey, you were certainly right about that," he said, his eyes twinkling. "They sure do know how to make a fish sandwich over there. Yes sir, that was about the best-tasting grouper I ever had! Why, the only way it could've been better would've been if I'd a' caught it myself!"

They both laughed long and hard at that.

After saying goodbye to Crabby Gus, AJ and Bodo continued home. When they pulled up to the house, AJ put his bike in the garage, then snuck around the corner and picked up the hose. He quietly turned it on, then peeked into the garage to see Bodo waiting patiently by the door to enter the house. AJ gave one sharp whistle and Bodo came bounding to him, to be greeted by a blast of water from the hose. Bodo jumped on him and the fun began. They wrestled around, with AJ having the advantage of the hose for a few minutes. They were finally interrupted when Hannah ventured out to see what the commotion was all about. "Hmm, well since you're already wet," she said, "the van could use a washing. I'll have lunch ready by the time you finish." AJ knew there was no escape. He went into the garage for a bucket, rag and soap and began to wash the van.

Minutes later he heard his father yell, "don't forget to do the inside." AJ rolled his eyes. So much for a lazy afternoon, he thought.

After finishing the van, AJ dried off Bodo and went in for lunch. Bodo went to nap on his bed and AJ spent the rest of the afternoon in his room playing video games.

That evening Rodger was planning to grill chicken for dinner. AJ eagerly offered to make Indian-roasted corn, one of his favorite foods. His dad had showed him how to make it. First he soaked the whole unpeeled ears in a bucket of water for an hour. Next, he carefully peeled back the leaves of the outer husks, removed the silk and spread the exposed cobs with butter, salt, pepper and secret spices, known only to him and his dad. Finally, he pulled the wet husks back tightly over the cobs, twisted them closed and placed them onto the grill.

Rodger grilled them until all sides were lightly charred. After they cooled a little, AJ peeled the husks back and twisted them tightly together, then tied a loose strip of husk around the twist to make a handle. The final result was impressive—a tray of steaming hot corn, glistening with butter, dotted with red and green herbs and filling the air with a wonderful roasted aroma. With the preparations complete, the family sat down to a wonderful dinner. AJ was especially proud of the corn.

When everyone was finished eating, AJ asked if he could give the left-overs to Bodo, to which his mother consented. AJ carefully picked the chicken from the bones and made a pile for Bodo. Rodger and Hannah grinned as they watched his appearance of serious concentration.

AJ then carefully sliced every kernel of corn off the last cob and mixed it in with the chicken.

"Here ya go, boy," he said, as Bodo wolfed it down.

After dinner the entire family relaxed in the living room, except AJ. He was back in the garage preparing for his trip to the beach. When he was ready to go, he told his parents where he was heading.

"Sabal Palms?" Rodger asked.

"Yep."

"Why don't you just go to our beach?"

"I've been there a thousand times, Dad. I feel like going someplace different."

"Well, I don't know, Son. That beach leads to Moccasin Head Point. That's where the troublemakers hang out at night."

"But, Dad, I promise to be back long before dark and I'll have Bodo with me."

Rodger couldn't argue with that. He knew that nothing would happen to AJ as long as Bodo was at his side. "OK Son, but be back before dark," he said sternly.

"I will, Dad," said AJ as he sped off on his bike, Bodo happily lopping alongside.

AJ wanted Bodo fresh when they arrived, so he took his time getting there. The parking lot at Sabal Palms Beach was much larger than the lots at Gulfside Beach and Sea Otter Cove. AJ rode his bike onto the sand and leaned it against a palm tree. As he began to survey the beach, he saw there were a few people scattered around but not enough to interfere with his work.

His plan was to search the main portion of the beach, then work his way toward Moccasin Head Point where he had seen large crowds of spectators during the fireworks display last night. On his scouting mission yesterday, he also noticed how the main beach was set up with a row of vendors along the area that backed up to the highway, selling every type of food, drink, toy and beach accessory imaginable.

Adjacent to that was a long row of rental tents. Visitors were lined up to rent beach chairs, umbrellas, rafts and giant tricycles with inflated tires that could ride across the water. Of course you had to watch out for the wind surfers skirting the beach and the skim-boarders sliding along the water's edge.

He also made note of how the covered pavilion area had been taken over by a local band having an impromptu jam session, the surrounding area becoming a dance floor.

There was also a volleyball area that was divided into four courts. As AJ was deciding where he was going to begin his search, he noticed a familiar face in the distance. It was Maximillion Mumpford and he was not alone. He was holding a short leash, attached to one of the scruffiest little terrier-type dogs AJ had ever seen.

"Why, hi there, young fellow," yelled Maximillion in friendly greeting.

"Hi, Mr. Mumpford, I see you got yourself a dog," said AJ with his eyes wide.

The prospector beamed with pride, "That's right. I rescued him from the pound. The fellow there said he was gonna' be put down the very next morning. He said the owners gave him up because he wouldn't stop digging holes in their yard. When I heard that, I said to myself why that's the dog for me! The fellow also said he was real smart," he said with a wink and a nod to AJ, alluding to their shared secret.

"That's great, Mr. Mumpford," said AJ, getting down on his knee to pet the scruffy animal who appreciated the attention, but kept a wary eye on the big red dog. "What's his name?"

"Miner," said the Prospector, smiling lovingly down at the mangy, gray, wire coated dog.

AJ laughed. "How's he doing?"

"Well, actually I was kinda' hoping you might offer a fellow some pointers."

"Sure," said AJ, "show me what he can do." AJ then walked with Bodo to the shade of a cluster of palm trees and settled down in the sand to observe. Maximillion picked up his metal detector in one hand, and with the dog leash in the other, set off walking slowly, sweeping the detector back and forth across the beach. After about a minute, he got a "ping" and the dog jumped to attention. The prospector began to scratch the ground in the area of the "ping" while calling Miner's name. The dog quickly jumped in and with the digging fury only a terrier owner would understand, scooped out a sizeable hole in the beach in seconds. The prospector then sifted through the loose sand in the pile behind the dog, only to find a bottle cap.

AJ smiled as Maximillion then pulled a can of squirt cheese out of his back pocket. He rewarded Miner with a squirt, then looked back at AJ beaming with pride. "What'a ya think of that!" he said. "Now alls' I gotta' do is teach him the difference between gold and scrap metal and I won't need this here detector no more! And he sure saves me a whole lotta digging!" AJ didn't know quite what to say. It was clear the little dog didn't have a clue about tracking or detecting articles, but he certainly did know how to dig! It was also very clear that this scruffy little dog had found a soul mate in Maximillion Mumpford, just as Bodo had with him.

"I think he's doing great!" said AJ. "And like you said, he'll sure save you from doing all that digging."

"That's right," said the old hippy with a huge grin. "I just knew he was real smart."

"Well, good luck to you both, Mr. Mumpford. Goodbye Miner," said AJ, as he headed on his way.

"So long, Son. Happy hunting!"

Because Maximillion was already searching this beach, AJ decided to alter his plan as a courtesy to the senior prospector and search Moccasin Head Point first. He would search the main beach area later. He had no idea of the far-reaching consequences that one simple decision was about to have.

AJ decided the best way to search this area was to start out on The Point, the peninsula of land that jutted out from the main beach. From there he would work his way back down Pirate Bones Path, the thin strip of land connecting The Point to the beach. He was thinking of what his father said about the troublemakers hanging out there after dark, so he planned to finish as early as possible.

The entire peninsula was a popular destination for boaters. All day yesterday, party boats had come and gone, mooring at the west end and coming ashore to picnic or swim in the cool Gulf waters.

AJ started at the very tip and guided Bodo back and forth across the peninsula, his pattern widening as the land itself widened. The pair had searched almost the entire peninsula with no luck. AJ looked around to review the situation and noticed a very large rock along the southern edge of the peninsula. The rock was large enough to lounge on. His prospecting sense told him to search along all sides of the rock. He steered Bodo in that direction, and sure enough, Bodo alerted. AJ had to bend over and look clear under the overhanging portion of the rock to find the object. What he saw was a small cloth bundle. He carefully reached far under the rock to grab it. The cloth was a blue and white bandanna. He unwrapped it. Inside the bandanna he found a beautiful gold watch, imbedded with what appeared to be diamonds. The bandanna was very worn, with one corner beginning to fray badly. His first thought was someone must have stashed it here while they took a swim, then left without it. From his vantage point on the rock, AJ could see for miles in all directions. There was not a boat in sight. As he turned the watch over, he saw writing in fancy letters on the back. It read, "*To CWP, MD, Love, Mom and Dad.*" AJ was overcome with emotion. He knew this watch was by far the most valuable item he had found. He also knew that somebody somewhere was heartbroken over losing it.

He began to feel that familiar surge of conscience rise up in his stomach again, the one he felt every time he thought about the people who owned the objects he found.

He decided he should start looking in the lost and found section of the newspaper occasionally, just in case. He had once found a kitten in his backyard and his mother had scoured the lost and found listings for a week before finally spotting the ad that eventually reunited the little kitten with its owner.

Yeah, that's what I'll do, he thought. His conscience now fully soothed, he carefully rewrapped it in the cloth bandanna and dropped it into his shirt pocket. As he spun around to go, he looked up to see Billy Bozwell glaring down at him. A wave of anger and fear swept over him. Bozzy was purposely blocking Pirate Bones Path, his only means of escape. AJ was certain Bozzy had seen him find the watch. His heart was racing—Bozzy took a single step sideways to make sure AJ knew he was not getting past him.

"I see you found my watch, punk" he said, with a heavy threat in his voice. "Give it back, now!"

"Your watch?" said AJ, anger rising up as he remembered the humiliation of last night.

"Yea, that's right, my watch," said the thug. "I put it there to take a swim."

AJ knew the watch was not Bozzy's. He didn't think Bozzy could even tell time. "Well, before I hand it over, you have to identify it," said AJ.

"It's a gold man's watch, with a gold band, now give it to me you little loser!" Bodo, who had to this point been cautiously observing, attempted to maneuver himself between AJ and the bully, but AJ held his lead tight.

"All you have to do is tell me what it says on the back of the watch. If you can, I'll give it to you."

"Oh, I'll tell you what it says, you little geek," sneered Bozzy. "It says either you give it to me right now or I'm just gonna' have to take it from you!"

"Well—ah, actually—" AJ stammered, gathering his courage to make a stand. "That's not what it says, so I think I'd better try to find its real owner."

He then attempted to walk around Bozzy. As he tried to slide past him on the narrow walkway, he felt a painful grip on his shoulder as Bozzy grabbed him. But he didn't feel it for long. Bodo instantly reacted. He reared up and grabbed Bozzy by his leather-clad elbow with his powerful jaws, the same arm Bozzy was restraining AJ with, and yanked the arm off AJ, setting him free.

Bozzy fought back. He swung his free fist at Bodo's head, but missed. Bodo yanked in the opposite direction to avoid the blow and to pull the attacker off balance, exactly as Ivo had taught him through countless hours of patient and diligent training. Next Bozzy tried to kick the dog, but again Bodo easily sidestepped every attempt, still keeping his hold on the elbow through the black leather jacket.

AJ watched, frightened, his mind racing. Bozzy was cursing and screaming at Bodo, and Bodo answered with deep, guttural growls. Bozzy attempted one final kick to Bodo's head. Bodo again yanked him hard in the opposite direction causing him to fall to the ground. AJ was seeing for the first time the full extent of strength, sheer courage and fighting drive Bodo possessed.

Finally realizing he was hopelessly pinned, Bozzy stopped struggling and yelled, "Get it off! Get this stupid mutt off me!"

At that instant, AJ yelled, "*Aus!*" and Bodo released immediately, as he was trained to do. He then slowly began to circle Bozzy carefully to be sure he didn't lash out again.

Seizing the opportunity, AJ called to Bodo, and together they took off for AJ's bike with lighting speed. It seemed like an eternity passed before they finally reached it. He jumped on and pedaled as fast as he could, Bodo running alongside.

As they took off, AJ kept looking over his shoulder to see if Bozzy was following them. Bozzy emerged from the path covered in sand and grasping his elbow. As they sped away, he yelled to AJ, "This ain't over yet, you little punk, this ain't over!"

As AJ raced through the parking lot past Bozzy's motorcycle, he stopped to pick up the lead that was dangling behind Bodo.

"*Geh weg!*" he yelled, deciding to let Bodo do the work. They needed to get out of there fast! It would be harder for Bozzy to follow them if they took the side streets home, which they did.

By the time he reached his house, AJ had calmed down somewhat. He wanted to tell his dad what had happened, but he was afraid. He had been warned, and his dad was right. If he told him, he would probably not be allowed to venture far from home for a long while. And besides, what exactly would he tell him about the gold? How could he explain to his parents how Bodo found the gold watch without revealing everything he'd been up to the entire summer? Something told him his parents would not approve.

He went to his room and dropped the watch, still wrapped in the bandanna, into his peanut butter jar. Staring at the almost half-full jar, he debated. *Maybe I should tell them, but when, and how?* He knew he would have to pick the perfect time and he would need to have his explanation firmly in place before facing them.

Not tonight, he thought, *I've had enough trouble for one day.*

As he looked down at Bodo lying on the floor, he called him over and gave him a hug. "Thanks boy," he said. "I'm sure glad you were there!" Bodo responded by licking AJ's face while his tail wagged in circles. AJ went to watch television in the living room, while Bodo curled up in his beanbag bed.

AJ tried to concentrate on the show, but his mind kept wandering back to the attack. Bozzy's words haunted him. He tried to think of what he might do to get back at him and he was frightened. The incident would bother him all evening, until eventually, he fell asleep in front of the television. He was awakened by loud snoring from Bodo, who had rolled over in his beanbag bed to sleep on his back. AJ gazed down at the big red dog who had risked danger without a moment's hesitation to protect him. He reached over to pet the soft floppy ears, while Bodo snored peacefully without a care in the world.

CHAPTER TEN

Bozwell's Revenge

Rodger was studying the want ads over his second cup of coffee when he heard an urgent knock at the front door. Hannah had already left for work, the girls were still sleeping and AJ was in his room playing video games.

As he walked past the cuckoo clock, he noticed the time was nine-fifteen. He opened the front door to see two uniformed police officers standing there.

"Good morning, Sir, I'm Sergeant O'Conner and this is Officer Dempsky. May we please come in?" said the younger and friendlier of the two.

"My wife?" Rodger asked, alarmed. "Did something happen?"

"No, no, nothing like that, Sir," said Sergeant O'Conner, who Rodger recognized as the forces' only canine officer.

"We're here on a complaint," he said. "About a theft." Rodger's face went ashen.

"I'm afraid the charges are pretty serious," said the

older officer, gruffly handing Rodger the warrant. "It involves your son and his dog."

Rodger began to read the papers with trembling hands. The charges read, in part, that AJ stole the complainant's gold and diamond Rolex watch, which he had removed while he went swimming, and when he tried to get the item back, AJ ordered his dog to attack him. Rodger stared at the papers a moment in shock and was about to bellow for AJ, when he walked into the room.

"What's goin' on, Dad?" he asked, nervously, immediately recognizing Officer Dempsky. He had given AJ several warnings about Bodo being off leash in public.

"Son, this officer says someone has accused you of stealing a valuable watch and ordering Bodo to attack him when he attempted to get it back. I think you better tell me exactly what's going on."

"That's a lie!" AJ said, his heart beginning to pound, "I found it, Dad, it wasn't his! He's lying! I found it on the beach, under a big rock!"

"That's why we're here, Son. We need you and your father to come down to the station with us to make a statement," said Officer Dempsky. "And we're gonna' need that watch."

"Also, we need you to bring along the dog's shot records," added Sergeant O'Conner. "It's standard procedure in a dog bite complaint." AJ ran to his room for the watch. Rodger went to gather all the paperwork that had arrived from Germany with Bodo. Officer Dempsky offered to drive Rodger and AJ to the station, having noticed there was no vehicle in the driveway. Rodger accepted the offer but explained that he needed a minute to wake his daughters.

The officers waited while Rodger woke Becki and told her to watch Nixie for awhile, because he and AJ needed to go down to the police station to straighten out some kind of misunderstanding. Seeing her fear he added, "Honey, it's all right. It's nothing serious, it's just a mix-up. We'll be back before you know it."

During the ride to the station, AJ started to tell his dad everything, but the officers advised him to wait until he made an official statement at the station. Rodger was assured that he would be present during any questioning, since AJ was a minor.

Inside the drab and stuffy police station, Rodger and AJ were led to a small office with two desks. Officer Dempsky took Bodo's paperwork and left to walk it over to animal control in the building behind the station. Sergeant O'Conner took a seat behind one of the desks and motioned to Rodger and AJ to sit.

As the sergeant turned on the recording device, AJ

nervously removed the watch from his pocket and laid the bundle down in front of the sergeant, then took his seat.

Sergeant O'Conner picked it up carefully, unwrapped the bandanna and examined it, pausing for a long while to study the inscription. He turned it over and studied the front. The watch was very unique. It had a mother-of-pearl dial with a 14kt. gold rotating outer bezel. Diamonds set in gold marked off the hours. The writing on the face of the watch said "Oyster Perpetual Date, Yacht-master-Rolex." The Sergeant gently layed the watch down and looked up at AJ.

"Son," he asked, "do you have any idea how valuable this watch is?"

"No, Sir," said AJ. But Rodger did. The sergeant then opened a drawer and pulled out an evidence bag, and dropped in the watch along with the bandanna. After filling out the label, he began to read the charges aloud to AJ and Rodger.

When he was finished, he laid down the paper and picked up a pencil and waited. Rodger, upon hearing the name "Bozwell," felt the anger rise up in his throat as his hands tightly clutched the wooden chair arms to keep from shaking. "I should have known a Bozwell was involved," he said through clenched teeth. "And if my dog did attack him—I'll bet he deserved it!" Sergeant

O'Conner raised his hand to signify silence. Rodger sat back in his chair and fumed. The sergeant then reassured AJ that everything would be all right and asked him to tell him exactly what happened.

Just as Officer Dempsky returned to the room, AJ began his story, starting from the beginning so it would make sense. He explained how Bodo had found Becki's missing bracelet, how he then went on to teach Bodo to find gold and that so far this summer he had found about a half a peanut butter jar full of gold jewelry.

"You did what?" said Rodger, after AJ finished the part about teaching Bodo to find gold. "You mean to tell me Bodo can sniff out gold and you have a bunch of it stashed in a jar in your room?" he asked, his head now in his hands. Sergeant O'Conner again raised his hand to Rodger in a gesture to remain quiet.

"Please, Mr. Jenkins, I need to ask the questions."

"Sorry," said Rodger, again easing back into his chair.

"AJ," Sergeant O'Conner began, "do you mean to tell us that your dog can sniff out gold, and you have a bunch of it stashed in a jar in your room?" Rodger grinned in spite of the situation.

"Yes sir, it's true," said AJ.

"You mean that's what you have been up to all summer, all those walks on the beach, all this time?"

asked Rodger, still trying to comprehend the situation.

AJ nodded. "I'm sorry I didn't tell you sooner, Dad, I was afraid you might be angry."

"AJ," the Sergeant continued, "assuming that's all true, how does it tie in to what happened last night?" AJ went on to explain how he had been searching Moccasin Head Point when he recovered the watch, wrapped in a bandanna and stuffed under the big rock. After he placed it in his pocket, he turned around and saw Bozzy had been watching him the entire time. Bozzy demanded the watch and said he had left it there to take a swim.

"But he wasn't even wet or wearing a bathing suit. He still had his riding jacket on. I knew he was lying so I told him I would give him the watch if he could tell me what it said on the back."

"Sounds reasonable," said Sergeant O'Conner, nodding his head in agreement.

"He didn't know what it said, so I told him I was gonna' try to find its real owner." Then turning to his father, "I really was, Dad, I promise. I was planning on checking the lost and found in the paper . . ."

"Go on, Son," said Rodger, frowning.

"Well, Bozzy was standing there blocking the path, so I tried to go around him and he grabbed me by my shoulder and squeezed hard, really hard."

"What!" Rodger snapped. "That big oaf laid his hands on you! He's lucky it was Bodo there and not me, or you guys would be interviewing him from his hospital bed!"

"That's enough, Mr. Jenkins," said Sergeant O'Conner. "One more outburst and I'll ask you to wait outside. Your comments are not helping your son's case one bit!" Rodger, realizing he was right, tried to calm himself, but inside he was churning with rage. The thought of his fourteen-year-old son being pushed around by a six-foot two, two-hundred-and-eighty pound thug made him more angry than he thought possible.

"All right AJ, after Billy Bozwell grabbed you, what happened next?" Sergeant O'Conner asked calmly.

"Well," AJ began, "Bodo jumped up and grabbed Bozzy's arm through his leather jacket, the same arm he was holding me with." AJ then grabbed his own arm to demonstrate, "Then Bodo pulled Bozzy's arm off me and Bozzy tried to kick and punch Bodo but Bodo kept yanking him in the opposite direction until finally Bozzy fell down. Then I yelled *Aus* and Bodo let go. Then Bodo kinda' stood guard over Bozzy for a few seconds and I figured we better run for it. I called him to come and we ran out of there as fast as we could."

Sergeant O'Conner looked confused. "You yelled *Aus?*" he asked. AJ nodded. "But *Aus* is a German command?" AJ nodded again. "Why did you train your dog in German?"

"I didn't," AJ replied. "My Uncle Ivo did—in Germany—he was a famous Schutzhund trainer!"

"A Schutzhund trainer?" asked Officer Dempsky. "What kind of dog is a Schutzhund?"

Before AJ could answer, Sergeant O'Conner broke in. "Schutzhund training, Harry— it's a German dog sport and training system—A highly intensive program for working dogs, kinda' like the Navy Seals or the Green Beret. In fact, our canine Axel is a Schutzhund 3 dog, trained over in Germany before the force bought him." Sergeant O'Conner then turned to AJ, "Tell me Son, what level is Bodo?"

AJ looked down at his hands. "My uncle died before he ever trialed him." Then he added, "But we joined the Schutzhund Club in Osceola Springs and we're working towards his first trial for his Schutzhund 1 title now that he has his BH."

"Is that so. You say your uncle trained him?" Sergeant O'Conner asked, clearly intrigued.

"Yes, sir, before I got him." The two officers then asked Rodger and AJ to remain there while they left the room to discuss the situation.

AJ and Rodger sat alone waiting. "I'm real sorry, Dad,"

AJ said quietly.

"It's all right son. I know you didn't steal anything, and Bodo was just doing his job. We'll get it straightened out. But AJ, I sure wish you had come to me about this."

"I wanted to, Dad, but I didn't know what to tell you. About the gold, I mean. I just didn't know for sure if it was right. You know, keeping it all."

"Well, that's another issue we're gonna' discuss when we get home, but as far as Billy Bozwell goes, you and Bodo did nothing wrong. Bodo defended you after you were attacked, the same thing any good family dog would have done." Rodger then added, "I gotta' tell you though, son, that Bozwell kid is built like a Buick. I'm surprised Bodo was able to hold him."

AJ's face beamed with pride. "Aw, you should've seen him, Dad, he was great! He knew exactly what to do! He kept yanking Bozzy around to keep him off balance, just like we're learning in *sch* . . ."

"Shhh!" said Rodger, pointing to the tape recorder, not sure if it was still running.

"You know, Son, tonight I was going to grill five of my famous jumbo mushroom burgers. Now, I think I'm going to grill six. One just for Bodo."

AJ smiled. He was relieved his dad was taking it so well and he was starting to feel a little better.

After a few minutes, the two officers came back into the room. Sergeant O'Conner spoke first. "Son," he said, "that was a very interesting story you told us, and we want to believe you. But we are going to have to investigate a little further. You see, what we have here is, on one hand, a boy with a pile of gold he claims his dog found and on the other hand, Bozwell has filed charges of theft against you."

AJ began to get angry again. So did Rodger. "The best thing we can think of in your defense is to prove your claims that the dog can, in fact, detect gold. That would help explain why you had that watch in the first place and why you have half a jar of jewelry you claim you found on the beach."

Rodger jumped up, "Are you implying my son is a thief?"

"We're not implying anything, Mr. Jenkins. We just need to get to the truth. Now you must admit, your boy has made some unusual claims. You can't expect us to just accept everything he said without looking into it?" said Officer Dempsky. "But if the dog actually can do what the boy said, it would certainly make things a lot clearer."

"I guess you're right," said Rodger, desperately hoping Bodo really could find gold.

"I'll prove it, Dad, I will! Bodo finds gold all the time!"

said AJ.

"Well," said Dempsky, "that's kind of what we had in mind. How about we give you two a quick ride home to pick up the dog, bring him here and Sergeant O'Conner will administer and monitor a totally voluntary test, if you agree to it?"

"Sure!" said AJ, anxious to prove his innocence. "Dad, you'll see, Bodo can find gold anywhere!"

"Now, Son," warned Rodger cautiously, turning to face AJ. "We don't have to do this," he said looking deep into his son's eyes for the truth. "Unless you're absolutely sure?"

"I'm sure, Dad."

AJ rode in the back of the unmarked police car. When they pulled up, AJ ran in to get Bodo.

"AJ," pleaded Becki anxiously as he ran past her. "Please tell me what's going on?"

"I need to bring Bodo to the police station, to prove we're innocent!" he yelled over his shoulder as he raced to get Bodo's leash. "I'll explain everything when we get back. Don't worry," he added, when he heard Nixie start to cry. "Everything's gonna' be fine, I promise." Then he hastened Bodo out the door, loaded him into the back of the police car, and climbed in after him. Bodo was very happy to be going for a ride. AJ was silent the entire ride back to the station. He knew the most important test of his life was only minutes away.

As they headed back to the small office, Sergeant O'Conner explained how he wanted to test Bodo.

"In the large conference room down the hall, I've pushed the table out of the way to give us plenty of room. On the floor I placed four styrofoam cups about five feet apart, and I punched air holes in them. Then I put one item under each cup. I used a penny, a nickel, a quarter and my own gold wedding ring. We'll enter the room together, then when we call you, bring Bodo in and show us how he finds gold. Any questions?"

"No, Sir," said AJ confidently. "We're ready!"

They all walked down the hall and everyone entered the room except AJ and Bodo. After they took their places, Sergeant O'Conner called AJ in. AJ walked Bodo into the room, paused for a moment and then gave the command, "Bodo, find the gold!" Bodo immediately went to work, searching all the cups. There was no alert. "Find the gold!" AJ repeated, starting to get concerned. Bodo then began to circle the room, searching every inch of floor.

It was obvious to Sergeant O'Conner, a trained canine officer, that Bodo was not picking up the scent.

"C'mon', Son, make him do it," said Rodger, worry clearly visible on his face.

"I am, Dad," he said. "Let me try again. Bodo, find the gold!" Once again Bodo sniffed each cup and then moved past them to circle around the entire room. There was still no alert. "I don't get it," said AJ, anxiously. "Something's wrong."

Sergeant O'Conner went over to the cups and lifted them one at a time so AJ and Rodger could see that the test was fair. Sure enough, under the third cup, sat his gold wedding ring. "Mr. Jenkins, please take AJ and Bodo back into the office."

AJ and Rodger returned to the small office with Bodo, very disappointed and confused.

"I don't understand, Dad," said AJ, fighting back tears. He wouldn't let his father see him cry. "I'm telling you the truth. Bodo really does find gold on the beach, I promise!"

"I believe you, Son," Rodger said, "but it's not me you have to convince. It's those two guys in the blue uniforms and frankly, you're not off to a very good start."

"I know, Dad," AJ muttered, looking down at the grey speckled floor.

"Are you sure you gave the right command?" Rodger asked, trying to be helpful.

"Yes, it's the only command he knows to find gold."

The two of them just sat there in silence, trying to

figure out what was happening.

In the other room down the hall, the two officers were discussing the situation.

"Well, if the boy's lying about the dog," said Officer Dempsky, "maybe he did steal the jewelry?"

"I don't think so, Harry. If that were the case, wouldn't we have at least one report of missing jewelry?"

"Yeah, that's true, we've only had one report of stolen jewelry in the last six months. Ms. Buccannon and her diamond broach, remember?"

"Oh, yeah. It turned up a week later in her laundry basket," laughed O'Conner.

"No," continued Dempsky. "The only reports of theft lately have all been on the east side. You know, that East Side Prowler. That was everything but jewelry and we did get that one surveillance shot of the guy, and he was definitely not a kid. And another thing I don't get, Mike, if the boy is lying, why was he so anxious to take the test?"

"I don't know, Harry, but I do know one thing. I've seen that boy on the beach many times as I patrolled down Nature Coast Highway this summer. I saw him following behind that dog. I saw it with my own eyes. The dog was always wearing a tracking harness and a ten-meter lead and always going along with his nose to the ground. You couldn't help but notice them. I puzzled over it myself a few times. That dog was definitely tracking something, but what?" asked O'Conner. "It just doesn't add up. I mean, you and I both know Billy Bozwell didn't lose that watch. He probably couldn't even identify it in a line up of one!"

"Yeah, you're right there, so how did he just happen to be on the point at the exact moment the kid found it? To take a swim?" pondered Dempsky.

"No," said O'Conner. "That can't be. Like the kid said, he was fully dressed, still wearing his leather jacket, and a good thing too. Do you have any idea what kind of damage that dog could've done to a bare arm?"

"You're right there, it could have been a lot worse. I have to agree with you, it's too much of a coincidence. You think maybe he was coming back for it himself?" asked Dempsky.

"Knowing Bozwell, that's exactly what I think. I think he stole it, then stashed it there until he could get it later when the heat was off. But what I can't figure out is, if he did steal it, why would he get the police involved? Doesn't he realize we're going to find out if it was stolen?"

"Oh, I can answer that one," said Dempsky. "He didn't make the complaint. It was his father."

"Clinton Bozwell?"

"Yeah, he called it in. He was furious. Said his kid was covered in blood after being mauled by Rodger Jenkins's vicious dog. He said his son told him he bought the watch from some guy last week and took it off to take a swim, then caught the Jenkins kid stealing it red-handed. That's what he told his old man anyway."

"I didn't realize that big goon was still a minor," said O'Conner, thumbing through the report. "Well, not for long. Says here he's eighteen next month."

"OK, Mike, so let's say the kid is telling the truth. Then why did the dog fail the scent test?" asked Dempsky suspiciously.

"I don't know, but I intend to find out," said O'Conner, puzzled. His instincts told him AJ was telling the truth and he was determined to figure the mystery out. As he paced back and forth in the room, reviewing the facts over and over, Officer Dempsky broke the silence.

"Say, Mike, in all the time you've been working with dogs, have you ever heard of a dog that could sniff out buried gold?"

"No, Harry," O'Conner replied. "In fact, I don't even think it's possible, but I'm pretty sure that's not what's happening here."

"It's not?"

"No," said O'Conner, shaking his head, "Look, if I

command Axel to search a crime scene where I think a knife might have been discarded by a perp, the dog isn't actually searching for a knife. Instead, he'd be searching for the scent of the perp's interaction on an object, in this case, a knife. So what I figure is, Bodo is probably searching for the smell of human interaction on the jewelry. But I don't know what that interaction is," he pondered. "No," he said, shaking his head. "I do believe the dog is finding jewelry and that's the first part of the puzzle. I'm fairly certain I remember learning that pure gold has no scent. I mean, if it did, every prospector on earth would have a dog."

"Yeah, I'd be the first one in line down at the pound," laughed Dempsky.

"No, Harry," O'Conner continued. "It's not the gold he's smelling. It's something else. Now, from what I remember from my college chemistry class, almost all gold jewelry sold today is 14kt. Pure gold is 24kt. To make 14kt. they have to blend 14 parts of pure gold with 10 parts of other metals. I don't remember them all, but I know some of the common ones are copper, silver, nickel and even zinc."

"So, what does that mean?" asked Dempsky.

"Harry, do something for me. Close your eyes, and tell me what you smell."

"You're joking, right?"

"Work with me for a minute, will ya?"

"This better be going somewhere," mumbled Dempsky grudgingly as he closed his eyes. O'Conner reached into his pocket and pulled out some change. He then held up a penny under the old officer's nose. "OK, Harry, I have a handful of change. I'm going to hold a coin under your nose. Tell me what coin you think it is."

"Hmf," he said. "It's a penny." He then opened his eyes to see if he was right. He was.

"How about that!" he said, amazed that he had gotten it right.

"Now, you were able to do that with your pathetically weak, though oversized, human nose," said O'Conner, smirking. "Imagine what a well-trained tracking dog can do. Your schnoz has about five million scent receptors. I think a dog the size of Bodo would have somewhere around *two hundred million*."

"Go on," said Dempsky, intrigued.

"Here's an example of the power of the canine nose; Let's say you walk into a donut shop, something I've seen you do a few times. What do you smell? I'll tell you. You smell donuts. If Axel or Bodo walked into that same shop, they wouldn't smell just donuts, they would smell flour, eggs, sugar, yeast, cream, chocolate, they would even be able to smell what type of oil they were frying in. That's called *odor layering*, something dogs have the ability to do."

"Odor layering?"

"Right. In the eight years I've worked with canines, which includes my military canine background, I've seen dogs do some amazing things. I've seen dogs alert on nothing more than a *trace* of narcotics in a vehicle. I've seen the beagle brigade at the airport detect things as minute as a tiny cluster of fruit flies on a hidden piece of fruit, or contraband plant seeds buried deep in suitcases. I've seen search-and-rescue dogs find survivors buried under a ton of rubble. There have even been cases of dogs smelling cancer in humans. The canine nose is an incredible thing, Harry. Fact is, we may never understand its full potential. Now it's possible that Bodo is not really detecting gold per se. See, my theory is, he's probably detecting some sort of blend of the various metals and alloys that are used to make the 14kt. gold, combined with some element of human interaction. So, why did he fail to find my wedding ring?" he asked himself out loud.

"Maybe your wedding ring isn't real gold," laughed Dempsky.

"Very funny," said O'Conner. "Let's go back and question the boy again. I want to get to the bottom of this."

The officers re-entered the room where AJ and Rodger patiently awaited their fate. Bodo lifted his head and thumped his tail on the floor as they entered.

"AJ," began Sergeant O'Conner, "I want you to tell me *exactly* what was going on, the first time Bodo found jewelry. I believe you said it was your sister's bracelet?" AJ nodded. "And I need to know absolutely everything. What they were eating, drinking, wearing, doing. Leave out nothing, no matter how unimportant or insignificant you think it is, understand?"

"I understand," said AJ, seriously. "Becki, my sister, and her friend Pam were laying out on lounge chairs on the front lawn, sunbathing. I guess the sun must have moved because when I brought them their lemonade, they were picking up all their stuff and dragging it across the grass. I guess that must've been when the bracelet got lost."

"Ok," said O'Conner. "Describe the entire scene to me, every detail you can remember."

AJ closed his eyes tightly. "Well, Becki was sitting on the green lounge chair on top of a pink-and-white striped beach towel. She was wearing her old purple bathing suit. Pam was on the blue lounge chair with a white beach towel, wearing a bright yellow bikini, with white designs all over it and tie strings on the sides of both legs and on the top of her shoulders," he said with a grin.

"That was very observant of you," said O'Conner, clearing his throat. "Keep going."

"Well, it was before lunch, so I don't think they were eating anything. The radio was playing and I had just brought out two big, orange-colored plastic glasses of lemonade."

"Good. Now AJ, were they doing anything else, anything at all?

"I do remember some magazines on the ground, but no, I don't think they were doing anything but talking and listening to music."

"Hmm," said O'Conner. "Now when you decided to track for the bracelet, tell me exactly how you handled your dog."

"Well," he began, "I went and put on his tracking harness and clipped on his ten-meter tracking lead."

"Go on," said the sergeant, processing every detail mentally.

"Then, I looked around for something with Becki's scent on it. The only thing she had was the towel she'd been lying on. So I took the towel, let Bodo sniff it really deep and gave him the command, *Such*."

At that moment, Bodo picked his head up from its

resting place on the cool floor and looked up at AJ.

"No, Bodo," said AJ, petting his dog. Bodo put his head back down, flopped onto his side and stretched out.

"So, after he sniffed the towel, I gave the command and he started to sniff the ground. About a minute or two later, he seemed to lock onto a scent. He started heading over to where the girls were sitting before they moved and he lay down, which is his way of telling me he found something. I reached down deep into the sand under the grass and there it was!"

"Good. Now, after that incident, did Bodo just start finding gold immediately or did you have to work with him?" asked O'Conner.

"Well, I got to thinking about the stuff we were learning in my Schutzhund class, about tracking and imprinting, so I thought, maybe I could imprint him to find gold and we could search the beaches, just like the prospectors do with their detectors."

"And what did you use to imprint him with the gold smell?" asked sergeant O'Conner.

"I used the same bracelet he had just found," AJ said.

"Really," said O'Conner. "And how long a period of time passed from when you first found the bracelet and when you began to use it to imprint Bodo?"

"Maybe five minutes." AJ said, "Becki put it away so

she wouldn't lose it again, and I went in her room a few minutes later and borrowed it. Sorry, Dad," AJ said ashamed. "I know I should have asked her permission." Rodger had no response. He was simply numb. Nothing AJ could say now would surprise him. He just nodded.

"And after you worked with the bracelet, that's when Bodo started finding gold on the beach?" asked O'Conner.

"Well, I used the bracelet a few more times for practice but I didn't try him on the beach without it until about two weeks later. I had to wait for school to let out. I'm not allowed on the beach on school nights. But Bodo found gold the very first day we set out," said AJ.

"So, that's what you were doing all those times I saw you walking the beaches, day after day?" Rodger felt a pang of guilt upon hearing that even the local police knew more about his son's activities then he did.

"Yes, sir. We've been at it all summer."

Sergeant O'Conner got up from his seat and started to pace with his arms folded, muttering to himself. "There has to be something. Human interaction—sand, salt, air, mixed with something—alloys, copper . . ." Then he stopped his pacing and whirled around toward the door and left the room.

He reappeared after a few very long minutes and said,

"Could everyone please follow me back to the other room." They all rose to go.

Everyone filed back into the large conference room except AJ, who hesitated outside the door. "You too, AJ," he said, smiling slightly.

Reassured, AJ entered the room. The four cups were still standing there.

"AJ," said the sergeant, "I want you to try again. Give Bodo the command." AJ looked up at him nervously, took a deep breath and turned to Bodo. "Find the gold!" he commanded. Bodo went right to work. When he checked the second cup, he alerted, lying down with the cup between his big paws. Sergeant O'Conner was smiling very broadly now and nodding his head.

"Go ahead, AJ," he said, "lift up the cup." AJ, afraid of another disappointment, hesitated for a moment. He walked over to the cup and nervously picked it up, revealing perhaps the most thrilling gold find of his life. The gold wedding ring was sitting there. Everyone was baffled.

"Now, we have to repeat this once more, to make sure it wasn't a fluke," said the Sergeant. He sent only AJ and Bodo out of the room as the others watched him hide the ring behind the trashcan in the corner of the room.

"AJ, come in," he yelled, as he sat on the edge of the

desk by the door. AJ entered this time with far more confidence and gave the command, "Find the gold!" Bodo quickly searched all the cups, then, finding nothing, began circling the room.

AJ was getting very nervous as Bodo moved away from the cups. As Bodo approached the trashcan in the corner, he lay down trying to put the can between his paws and knocked it over, exposing the ring. AJ grinned from ear to ear and got down to praise his dog. Rodger let out the breath he didn't realize he was holding, and Officer Dempsky just stood there scratching his head in confusion.

"All right," said Dempsky. "I don't get it. You mean the dog passed? He really can smell gold?"

"Well," said O'Conner, grinning. "Not exactly." They all looked at him puzzled. As he rose from the edge of the desk, he reached into his back pocket, and tossed onto the desktop a small tube of suntan lotion he had borrowed from one of the girls in the office.

"What's that for?" asked AJ.

"That, my young friend, is the smell I believe you imprinted on your dog!"

"What?" said everyone at once.

"That's right," said O'Conner. "Something in the lotion, maybe the cocoa butter, PABA, or something else, combined with one or more of the other metals in the jewelry, is probably what Bodo has been searching for. My guess is that your sister and her friend were wearing suntan lotion that day."

"Wearing it," laughed AJ. "They both were slathered in it. In fact, maybe that's why the bracelet slipped off in the first place!"

O'Conner continued. "When Bodo smelled the towel, the scent of suntan lotion was predominant. That became what he was searching for! Then, you used the same bracelet to imprint Bodo with the smell of gold, or in this case, 14kt. gold jewelry. Bodo was imprinted all right, but since the jewelry you used was heavily tainted with suntan lotion, Bodo was actually searching for 14kt. gold that had suntan lotion on it."

"You know what," said AJ. "That explains why Bodo never found any jewelry in the splash zone. The salt water must have washed off the suntan lotion."

"Well," said Officer Dempsky, "I have to say, I've never seen anything like this before and I've sure seen a lot of things in my life. A dog that can actually find gold, imagine that!"

"Only if the owner wore suntan lotion!" laughed AJ.

"Well, let's get you guys home," said Sergeant O'Conner. "I think we're through here for now. I'm going to recommend to the chief that we dismiss the theft complaint as unfounded. I'm convinced Bodo found the watch."

Officer Dempsky, who had just taken a call on the phone at the desk, interrupted. "I'm afraid they can't leave just yet—there's a problem. That was Bozwell's attorney. Seems he has decided to press charges."

"What does that mean?" asked Rodger.

Sergeant O'Conner looked troubled. "What it means," he explained, "is that under the county's Vicious Animal Ordinance, I'm afraid we have no choice but to confine the dog. I'm sorry."

"But I thought you said the charges would be dropped?" asked Rodger, running his hand through his hair in frustration.

"Yes, I did, but that was the theft charge. I'm convinced your son found that watch, but if they press charges on the attack, that's another issue altogether. I'm bound by law to restrain the animal until it's resolved."

"Resolved?" asked Rodger. "What does that mean?"

"It means it will have to go before a judge. Do you know a good lawyer you can call?" asked the Sergeant.

Rodger sat down hard and put his head in his hands.

"Mr. Jenkins," said O'Conner softly. Rodger looked up, "I'm afraid we need to take the dog now."

"Dad, no!" cried AJ, clutching Bodo's leash tightly to his chest. "No. Please Dad! You gotta' do something. They can't take him, I won't let them!"

AJ felt his eyes filling with tears. Sergeant O'Conner was disgusted with what he was being forced to do, but it was his duty to uphold the law. He also knew that something wasn't right about this whole case. He needed to get to the bottom of it and he knew exactly where to start. He had to find out where that watch came from.

"Son," said Rodger, holding AJ by the shoulders, "Listen to me. We have no choice. We need to leave Bodo here for now. As soon as we get home, I'm going to call a good lawyer. I promise, we'll do everything we can but we have to obey the law. Bodo will be all right." He could feel AJ's thin shoulders trembling.

Sergeant O'Conner turned to Officer Dempsky, "Harry . . ." The officer gently pried the leash from AJ's clenched hands and solemnly led Bodo out of the office. AJ watched them go with tears streaming down his face, then followed them out of the room to watch as they made their way down the long hallway. Rodger and the Sergeant continued to talk. As Officer Dempsky reached the end of the hallway and was about to turn the corner, AJ suddenly ran down the hall toward them. "Bodo!" he cried, "I'm sorry Bodo, I'm so sorry. Pleeeease don't take him, pleeeease!"

As he ran past an open office, young Officer Cooper was, at that instant, stepping into the hall. He collided with the hysterical boy and caught him around the waist, sweeping him off his feet and restraining him. AJ screamed and kicked to get free, and Bodo responded.

He turned and lunged in the direction of the rookie officer now holding AJ on his hip under one arm. The only thing between the terrified officer and Bodo was the iron grip Officer Dempsky had on the leash, but each lunge pulled him closer. Rodger and Sergeant O'Conner rushed into the hall in time to see the trembling rookie reaching for the flap over his gun. He had no intention of being attacked. As he fumbled with his holster, Rodger dove past him to put himself between Cooper and Bodo. Bodo was inching closer with each powerful lunge, violently snapping and snarling. He strained and pulled with every ounce of life and breath he possessed to defend his young master.

"Take your hands off the boy!" screamed Sergeant O'Conner. "Cooper, put the boy down!—I said let him go now!!!"

The terrified rookie finally understood and dropped AJ. AJ scrambled to his feet and ran to Bodo, who instantly stopped charging and just stood there licking

AJ's face. Young Cooper, still shaking, leaned against the wall to recover, his heart pounding, his trembling hand trying to redo the clasp on the flap over his gun. O'Conner snapped at him, "What did you think you were doing, Cooper?"

"The boy was running past me screaming, sir. I thought he, I thought he needed to be stopped. Then the dog started to charge me and . . ."

"The dog was protecting the boy, you fool, couldn't you see that!" yelled O'Conner, pacing angrily. "He's a trained protection dog and you were manhandling his master! What did you expect him to do, just stand there and watch? What do you think Axel would do if you tried to lay a hand on me?"

"I'm sorry, sir. I didn't realize, " the rookie mumbled.

"So you reach for your gun!" shouted the sergeant. "I'll deal with you later, Cooper. Get back to work."

"Yes, sir. Sorry sir." Cooper turned, shamed-faced, and slunk back into the office.

The Sergeant walked over to Rodger. "I'm sorry Mr. Jenkins, he's new. He never should have grabbed your son. I'm very sorry about that."

Rodger stood there wiping the sweat off his forehead. "Is this going to make things even worse for my dog?"

"Absolutely not," insisted the sergeant. "As far as I'm

concerned, that dog performed exactly as any loyal dog should. If we weren't standing here in this particular situation, I'd say you should be very proud of the way he protected your son. Now, maybe we should have your son bring him over to Animal Control."

"I think you're right," said Rodger. Then, turning to AJ, who had his arms locked around Bodo's neck, and tears still on his face, he said, "Come on, Son, it's time for Bodo to go."

CHAPTER ELEVEN

THE RAID

Hannah pulled the van into the garage. Her shift had ended at three o'clock and she was exhausted. It had been an extremely difficult day. One of her favorite residents had died. Pearl Parker had been under Hannah's care for almost six years, having been a resident of Gulfside Manor since the age of ninety-three and having outlived everyone she had known, including most of her own doctors. Hannah had come to adore the tiny black woman with the huge and knowing eyes.

Pearl loved to talk about her life growing up in Louisiana and about her five children, who were all now gone. Hannah would miss her.

With a heavy heart, she climbed out of the van and opened the back door.

She knew in half a heartbeat that something was very wrong in her home. She instinctively scanned the room for her children. AJ and Rodger were sitting at the table with very long expressions on their faces. "Where are the girls?" she asked, worriedly.

"In their room," answered Rodger, knowing she sensed trouble, and marveling at that mysterious thing called women's intuition. "They're fine, Hannah," he added, seeing the concerned look still there. Hannah always knew when something was wrong.

"Where's Bodo?" she asked, suddenly aware of the giant emptiness of his absence. He should have greeted her at the door with his tail wagging and his eyes sparkling.

"Honey, come and sit down and we'll explain everything."

"Is he hurt?" she asked, fearing the worst.

"No, no, he's fine. Please Hannah, sit down." She did.

Rodger began with the incident on the Point and Bodo's detainment. He then paused to give her time to process the information that her dog was locked up, her son had been accused of theft and they were very likely about to be sued. She sat there quietly listening. When she finally spoke, it was to AJ.

"AJ," she began patiently. "How is it you happened to find an extremely valuable watch that was hidden under a rock and wrapped in a bandanna?"

AJ swallowed hard and began. He then told his mother everything about Bodo learning to find gold, his daily excursions on the beaches and finally about the peanut butter jar, which he then produced from his lap. He placed it on the table, and nervously awaited his mother's response.

Hannah stared coldly at the jar, then back at her son. She then reached out, picked up the jar and dumped its contents onto the table. She began to pick up the jewelry piece by piece. Spread before her was a large assortment of gold bracelets, a 1989 class ring along with six other rings, many broken chain necklaces, a wedding band, several gold earrings, ankle bracelets, a pile of loose charms and a tiny locket with a photo of what appeared to be someone's mother in it. When she was finished she turned to her very nervous son. "And just what were you planning to do with all this?" she asked calmly.

"I didn't know," answered AJ. "I couldn't figure out what to do with it."

"AJ," she said. "Why did you keep this a secret?"

AJ put his head down. "I guess, because I knew it was wrong, but I wasn't sure."

"So, instead of talking to us to find out, you decided to just keep on finding things that other people had lost and hiding them in your closet?" AJ realized how bad it sounded when put that way, and hung his head even lower. "Yes, ma'am."

"Well," said Hannah calmly, "in light of everything that happened today, what do you now think about all this?" She passed her hand over the pile of jewelry spread across the table.

"I wish I'd never found it," AJ said as tears filled his eyes. "I just want Bodo back."

Rodger now spoke. "Son, I promise you we'll do everything we can to get Bodo back but what I think your mother is asking you, is what you plan to do with all this jewelry."

"I guess, at first I thought I could just keep it, like Maximillion does. He finds all kinds of stuff and he just keeps it. But then I kept remembering how Becki felt when she lost her sweet sixteen bracelet. It wasn't just a piece of gold to her. It was special. It meant something. If I found coins, well they would just be coins, nothing special. But I think jewelry is different. I think I'd like to try and find the people who lost these things and give them back."

Hannah smiled. "I'm glad to hear you say that, Alec Joseph, because that's exactly what you're going to do. First thing in the morning, you are to march right down to that police station and turn all this stuff in. If they want to look for the owners, fine. If not, they can give it to charity, for all I care. I just don't want it in my house. It's far too valuable, and the next thing you know, someone might try to break in here to steal it. I won't have my family put in danger over a pile of gold jewelry."

"Yes, Ma'am," said AJ, beginning to perk up at the thought of going back to the station and seeing Bodo.

Sergeant O'Conner sat staring at the inscription on the back of the Rolex watch: "*To CWP, MD, Love, Mom and Dad.*" The watch was called the Yacht-Master. *Well, let's start there*, he thought. He could have contacted the company and had them trace the serial number, but he thought he could find it faster himself. He turned to his computer and pulled up the state records of all the active boat registrations. In the state of Florida there were more than eight-hundred-thousand, with about five-thousand in Gulfside County.

He scanned the list starting with the "P's". It didn't take long to find who he was looking for; Dr. Charles Waylon Pennywell, Mayor Pennywell's son. "That's interesting," he said aloud.

"What's interesting?" answered Officer Dempsky

from the other desk.

"I think I found out whose watch this is."

"Who's?" asked Dempsky.

"Charlie Pennywell's."

"The mayor's son?"

"I think so," said O'Conner as he picked up the phone.

Charlie Pennywell was a very polite, tall, slightly built young man, fresh out of medical school. He was sitting across from Sergeant O'Conner who was now taking his statement.

"So you didn't realize your watch was missing until I phoned you?"

"Yes, Sir, that's correct," he said, sliding his glasses up a little. "I know exactly where I left it. I put it in the drawer in the cabin of my boat when I went for a swim. I forgot to put it back on. I assumed it was still there, until you called."

"And you had your boat out on the Fourth?"

"Yes, all day, with five friends. We spent the entire day on the water, except for the two hours we spent moored off of Moccasin Head Point. My girlfriend was getting sea-sick so we disembarked for lunch, to give her a chance to settle her stomach."

"And what time was this?" asked the sergeant.

"I would say around one o'clock."

"Was there anyone else on the Point while you were there?"

"Oh, yes, there were a lot of people. I'd say maybe thirty, but not together, in small groups, you know, spread out," he answered.

Then, just to be thorough, the Sergeant asked, "Do you remember seeing a boy around fourteen, with dark curly hair, very thin, kind of small for his age, maybe with a big red dog?"

The young man thought a minute. "No, I can't really say for sure, but definitely no big dog, that I would remember. My girlfriend is terrified of big dogs," he answered.

The Sergeant asked a few more questions, and then, as is standard procedure, asked for proof of ownership. All Rolex watches come with documentation and serial numbers. The young man looked up from his watch. "My parents gave it to me when I graduated med school. They were so proud. But sergeant, can I ask, do you know who stole it?"

"We don't have all the facts yet, but I'll let you know when we've sorted them all out. I'm sorry I can't release the watch to you now, but it's safe here until we wrap up this case," said the sergeant as the young man rose to leave. "Oh, by the way, do you remember if you were wearing sunscreen or suntan lotion that day?"

The young man looked puzzled. "Yes," he answered. "I burn easily. But why would you need to know that?"

"It's a long story," sighed the sergeant. "Oh, just one more question. Do you happen to own a blue-and-white bandanna?"

"No, I don't," said the young doctor. As he headed to the door, he paused, then turned around and spoke. "But I do remember someone on the Point that day who was wearing a bandanna like that."

Sergeant O'Conner walked the young doctor to the door. After shaking hands, they parted. He was delighted with the information he had been given. The description of the man on the Point matched Billy Bozwell. He didn't have enough to charge him yet but he knew he had his man. Officer Dempsky entered the room carrying two coffees and two bear claws and put them down on his desk. He handed one of each to O'Conner who propped his feet up on his desk and smiled at Dempsky with a smug look on his face.

"What's up with you?" asked Dempsky.

"We got him!" he said. "It was the bandanna. He was spotted wearing the bandanna!"

Dempsky broke into a wide grin, "We got him! The East Side Prowler?"

"No, the Rolex thief. He was—" at that instant both men simultaneously threw down their pastries and swung around to their computers.

They each pulled up the surveillance photos captured by the ATM, of the East Side Prowler. It was the only lead they had in a very notorious crime spree sweeping the east side of the county. And they each saw it at the same instant. The photo showed a man in a black skull cap, pulled way down over his hair and eyebrows. Tied across his lower face was the exact same blue-and-white bandanna they were now holding as evidence, with the frayed corner clearly visible in the photo.

"Woo Hoo!" they yelled to each other as they slapped hands in the air. "We got him!"

This was one of the most important cases they had dealt with in years. The pressure from the mayor's office to catch this crook was considerable, and their chief had been bearing down hard on them for weeks. They were ecstatic. They now had almost everything they needed to crack this case.

"Let's get that warrant!" said O'Conner as he sat back to enjoy his coffee.

The next day was Saturday. The warrant would be served on the Bozwell estate before first light. Sergeant O'Conner was disappointed that he could not be there. He had to leave town. He was required to attend a canine certification session annually with Axel. This year it was in Miami. It couldn't have fallen at a worse time, but he had no choice in the matter. Dempsky would lead the raid. They set out with Dempsky and Chief Martin in the lead car with two marked cars trailing as back up.

The Bozwell estate was situated high on a bluff overlooking the Gulf. A stucco wall topped with terra cotta tiles surrounded the entire estate. A large, white double-wrought-iron gate stood guard at the entrance to the driveway. Dempsky got out of the car and pushed the buzzer. It was a long time and a lot of rings before he finally got a response.

"Who is it and what do you want?" asked a rough man's voice over the intercom.

"Gulfside police, sir. We have a search warrant," began Officer Dempsky.

"A what?" shouted the dour voice.

"A search warrant to—"

"I heard you the first time. I'll be right down," snapped the voice and the intercom went silent. They waited for a few moments and finally saw the headlights of a green Hummer approaching from inside the gate. The driver got out. The man approaching was stout, tall, middle-aged and wearing a robe over trousers and shoes without socks.

Cliton Bozwell walked with a determined, arrogant stride to stand face-to-face with the officers.

"A warrant, you say. Let me see it," he demanded.

As he read the warrant, he began to stomp back and forth demanding to know what this was all about.

"Open the gate, sir," demanded the Officer.

"I'm calling my attorneys," shouted Bozwell.

"That's certainly your right, sir, but I have to insist either you open this gate or we will!"

The agitated man cast the papers onto the ground with venom and stomped over to the control panel. As the gates slowly creaked open, Dempsky got back in the car and sped through, passing the Hummer and the man, on the doublewide driveway. One officer stayed behind to escort Bozwell.

They sped down the long, circular, stone-paved driveway lined on each side with Pindo palm trees. The mansion was a sprawling and majestic Spanish Mediterranean style with terra cotta roof tiles topping classic white stucco walls and turrets. Summer flowers in full bloom lined the perfectly manicured walkways, which branched off the main path that led through an arched entryway to the main entrance. In the center of the driveway stood a majestic fountain surrounded by Sago palms, shrubs and more summer flowers in full bloom. Rising from the middle of the circular fountain was a pair of stone lions locked in battle. Dempsky began designating orders, and Chief Martin hung back to observe.

The items they were searching for were small, high priced electronics stolen from stores and warehouses throughout the East Side over a seven-month period.

The perpetrator had proven to be very cunning. He never left behind a single fingerprint and except for the happenstance of the ATM machine situated catty-corner from the last place he hit, they had no evidence.

From those stills, they learned that he was working alone and they had gotten a general description of body size, type, build and appearance, but still no smoking gun until the breakthrough with the bandanna.

The judge had been reluctant to issue the warrant until he was shown the sworn statement by the mayor's son, identifying Clinton's son Billy as the man with the bandanna that had turned up wrapped around Pennywell's Rolex.

Clinton Bozwell threw around a lot of weight in this town, but so did Waylon Pennywell. The pressure on the mayor to stop this crime wave was building daily. The warrant had been issued.

"You four go around the back and begin searching the out-buildings," ordered Dempsky.

The search had taken less than forty-five minutes. In a second story loft over the poolhouse, in a locked storage room, it ended.

Floor-to-ceiling boxes of palm pilots, DVD players, digital cameras and expensive laptops lined the walls and a stash of over seventeen-thousand dollars in cash was uncovered in a strongbox hidden inside an air-conditioning vent.

Dempsky personally slapped the cuffs on, while reading the suspect his rights, in the presence of his father, who looked on with an icy stare.

Clinton Bozwell was outraged that his son could be so stupid as to stoop to common burglary. He blamed himself at first. He had always planned to bring the boy into the business, to teach him the more subtle roads to wealth that existed for a man ruthless and cunning enough to take the risk.

There are many legal ways to pick a man's pocket and then have him thank you for it, and he had learned them all. The Bravetti Shipyard had been the Holy Grail to him. It represented everything he had aspired to in life. The prestige of owning the most respected yacht manufacturing plant on Florida's West Coast was irresistible. He loved the power, the hob-knobbing with the upper crust, the East Coast old money society, the lavish country clubs, the chauffeurs, the staff of live-in gardeners, cooks, maids and servants, the diamonds and jewels he decorated his wife with. It had all been within reach until the investigation by the Coast Guard. He spat on the ground at the memory.

The cost of the shipyard was more than he should have risked. He was far too extended going in, but he was blinded by greed and desire, certain that he could rake far more profit out of the operation than the two brothers had. How stupid they had seemed to him, living such modest lives, spending far more on each boat than he thought necessary and taking so little for themselves.

He had begun his usual routine of cutting costs immediately.

At every turn, it was Jenkins who had fought him. Jenkins—demanding better quality, better materials and more inspections. Jenkins—always Jenkins! He should have fired the man right off, but he needed him. When it came to boats, Clinton Bozwell didn't know stem from stern. No, he had needed Rodger Jenkins. And now everything in his world was collapsing. Scandal and ruination were all he could see. His son had been hauled off like a common street thug. Everything he had done had been for his two sons. Everything, good or bad, had been to hang onto the lifestyle he had provided for his family for so long. He would never go back. He couldn't. He had risked everything to rise up out of the shame of his immigrant father's ignorance and poverty. He vowed he would climb up society's ladder of wealth and power and never look back, whatever the price.

But now, everything was crumbling around him. Somehow, some way, he knew Jenkins was at the bottom of all this. First his shipyard and now his son. He had thought revenge was his when he ordered the Jenkins boy arrested for theft, but then, he had believed his son when he swore the watch was his. How stupid of his son to lie to him! Now he looked like a fool in front of the entire town. How inconceivable to risk everything over a watch! Now he was told that the burglaries had been linked to his son by a bandanna and all because that Jenkins kid had found the watch. It was more than he could bear. He would have his revenge.

"Watch your head," said Officer Dempsky, briskly, as he guided Billy Bozwell into the back of the patrol car. His father stood there frozen, seething with rage. He's taken my son from me, he thought. I'll take everything he has. As for his dog attacking my son, I'll sue him into bankruptcy and beyond and I'll see that dog dead if it's the last thing I do.

CHAPTER TWELVE

Fire!

The last Schutzhund trial that Ivo Bremik had competed in was many years ago. On that day, as Ivo had stepped onto the field with the legendary Cuno Von Bremik SchH3, Bodo's grandsire, his competition, fellow breeders and trainers alike, all stopped what they were doing and slowly made their way toward the field for a better view.

While it is common for fellow boxer breeders to watch a boxer compete, it is not common to see breeders of German shepherds, Belgian malinois and all the other working breeds make their way toward the field.

But they did and they were never disappointed. As Ivo and his dog left the field, his competitors marveled at the performance they had witnessed.

They knew perfection when they saw it and nodded their heads in agreement and commented about the enviable "Von Bremik" line, it's tremendous working ability, endurance, and especially it's courage. Bodo had inherited all these traits and they were soon to be tested in a very big way.

The convoy of police cars made their way back toward town. It had been a good day for the Gulfside Beach P.D. The Chief was delighted and as he dialed the number for the mayor's office, he knew the mayor would be also. Elections were just a few months away. Yes, it had been a very good day and it was not yet seven a.m.

They turned the convoy onto the Nature Coast Highway, just as Mayor Pennywell's voice came over the Chief's cell phone. "Well, Martin?" asked the mayor.

"We got him," answered the Chief.

At the Gulfside Manor nursing home, it had been a morning like most others. The residents had just finished their breakfast and were wheeled or escorted to the various activities that would fill their day. On the big open sun-porch that ran the length of the dining room in the back of the building, Miss Effie and old Henry Jones were sitting down to their usual morning game of checkers.

They were an unlikely pair. Miss Effie had taught first grade in Gulfside County for over forty years. There were very few people in town that had not had her as their teacher. She had taught three generations of many Gulfside Beach families, and was beloved by all.

She was also Mayor Pennywell's aunt. The mayor was a generous benefactor to the nursing home and visited often to be sure she received the best possible care. He doted on his kindly old aunt, who had taught him and all of his own children.

Meanwhile, old Henry had been a city worker all his life and like many men his age, had dropped out of school to help support the family. Now, the two had become fast friends.

"Miss Effie," said Henry, "I told you, you can't move in that direction. Remember, this is checkers, not Parcheesi."

"Oh, dear, Henry, am I doing it again?"

"That's all right, Miss Effie, just move it back and go forward this time," said the patient old man.

"Oh, I'm sorr—, Henry—what's that smell?" asked

Miss Effie, looking around her, concerned.

"I don't smell nothin', just coffee from the dining room."

"Oh, dear! I smell smoke!" Miss Effie said, as she stumbled out of her wicker chair. "Why didn't I hear the fire alarm go off? Oh dear, Oh dear. Someone has to warn the children!" She then tottered off quickly in the direction of the woods.

"Now Miss Effie, you come right back here right now!" yelled Henry.

"But I have to warn the children, Henry, I have to get them to safety!"

Henry had never seen her act this confused and became very alarmed. Henry was in a wheelchair and extremely frail. A nurse had wheeled him onto the sun porch and she would soon come to check on them, but he needed to tell someone now. The woods were only a few hundred feet from the back of the building, and Miss Effie was already disappearing from his blurred vision.

He tried to call out, but his voice was too weak to be heard above the clatter in the dining room as breakfast dishes were being cleared away. He pulled as hard as he could with his hands at the wheels of his chair to get moving. He rolled forward and knocked over the card table getting boxed in by its legs. He struggled desperately to move the heavy table to get free. It seemed several long minutes passed until Nurse Langley came around the corner and ran to help him.

"Mr. Jones!" she exclaimed, running to his aid, "Are you alright?"

"Miss Effie, Miss Effie," he shouted. "She ran into the woods to warn the children!"

"What children? Where is she?" she asked puzzled. "Warn them about what?"

"The fire! She thinks she's back in school. She went to warn the children! Hurry, Miss Terry, you've got to go get her!" he pleaded, frightened for his friend. Nurse Langley turned to look in the direction of the woods and panic filled her. The woods were on fire! She could see thick smoke rising in the distance. She ran inside and shouted to the other duty nurse to call 911, then ran outside toward the woods to find Miss Effie.

The police convoy was making its way back to the station with their suspect, slumped in the back seat, scowling. Suddenly a report came over the car radio.

There was a large brush fire in the woods behind the Gulfside Manor nursing home. A resident had wandered toward it, apparently confused or frightened. The fire was estimated to be less than a mile from the facility. "All units in the vicinity of the Gulfside Manor nursing home please proceed . . ." They threw on the sirens and sped to the scene.

Hannah was getting ready for work. She was due in for the early shift at the nursing home. "I don't want you walking the streets with a jar of gold jewelry under your arm, you might get mugged, or worse!" she said firmly to her anxious son.

AJ had been up since before dawn, waiting for the moment when he could bolt out the door to see Bodo.

"Your father will drive you. Now just sit still until I finish getting ready for work." He knew better than to push. He was already in enough trouble. He lay awake all night thinking of Bodo. It all seemed so strange to him. Just a few short months ago, he didn't even know the dog existed, and now, he couldn't imagine his life without him. He would gladly have given all the gold in the world if he could just get Bodo back.

Rodger had called around town looking for a lawyer as soon as he returned from the police station yesterday. He found one who was willing to talk to him, but not willing to take on the case. The woman told him that if the Bozwells succeed in proving the attack was unprovoked and excessively vicious in nature, the Gulfside County Vicious Animal Ordinance stipulates that the victim then had the right to demand the destruction of the animal.

Rodger had almost dropped the phone. He assumed there would be some sort of fine, but he never imagined Bodo could lose his life.

He did not tell Hannah or AJ. He couldn't. The lawyer also advised him that the Bozwells would probably pursue a personal injury lawsuit against him for damages occurring as a result of the attack, to strengthen their case. If they won the lawsuit, the case against the dog would be over. A judge, according to the ordinance, would likely uphold the verdict of the previous court and declare the animal "vicious." Clinton Bozwell could demand Bodo be destroyed.

As the three of them climbed into the van, Hannah saw the deep lines of worry on her husband's face. He had been unusually preoccupied since yesterday. She assumed the conversation with the lawyer had not gone well. AJ sat in the back of the van delighted that he was going to visit Bodo. In his back pocket was a new can of squirt cheese. He was planning to give Bodo the entire can. They headed in the direction of the nursing home to drop Hannah off at work and then planned to head to the police station to turn in the jar of gold jewelry and hopefully to visit Bodo.

As they drove down the Nature Coast Highway, they were forced to pull over for a line of police cars coming up from behind them with lights and sirens blaring.

"My goodness," said Hannah, concerned, "I wonder what's happening?"

After the police cars passed, they continued the remaining half-mile to the nursing home to discover where the police cars were headed. As they pulled in, they could see in the distance the rising gray clouds of a forest fire. The front entrance to the nursing home was chaos and confusion. The police cars had just pulled in ahead of them and were parked haphazardly around the circular driveway. Residents and nurses all moved about in a state of confusion. Rodger pulled the van over, well out of the way and they jumped out. Hannah ran ahead to find out what had happened. Rodger spotted Officer Dempsky beside his car and walked over to him. As he approached the car, he stopped, surprised to see Billy Bozwell glaring at him from the back seat, in handcuffs. Rodger was confused. Dempsky walked Rodger out of Bozwell's hearing and spoke, "He's under arrest for the east side burglaries, and by the way, I wanted to thank you."

"Me?" said Rodger.

"Yeah, if it hadn't been for your boy finding that watch, we would never have made the connection," said the Officer.

"What connection?"

"To the bandanna the watch was wrapped in."

"What's the connection?" asked Rodger.

"You know all those robberies over on the east side of town?"

"Yes, I've heard," said Rodger.

"We have a surveillance photo of the guy wearing the identical bandanna over his face."

The officer walked back to his radio to respond to a call. Rodger stood there trying to piece it all together. Bodo and AJ had accidentally led to the capture of the elusive East Side Prowler, who turned out to be Bozwell's kid! That definitely cleared AJ of the theft, but how did it affect Bodo? He was pondering all this when he saw Hannah running toward him.

"Oh, Rodger!" she cried "It's Miss Effie! She wandered into the woods! It's been over thirty minutes and they haven't found her!"

Ready to jump in and help search, Rodger ran back to the patrol car. At that instant the mayor pulled up in his official limo, which screeched to a halt next to the two men. He jumped out of the back and marched straight over to Officer Dempsky. "Did you find her yet?" he bellowed.

"No, Sir, not yet, but we have every available man out there looking." answered Dempsky. "I'm sure we'll find her any minute."

"See that you keep me informed. I want to know the second they find her!" Then, looking into the back seat, "Is that him?" he asked, nodding in the direction of the squad car.

"Yes, sir, and by the way, this is the man you have to thank," he said, pointing to Rodger. "It was his son who found your boy's Rolex watch, which eventually led us to him," nodding toward the car.

"That so?" said the mayor, turning to look at Rodger, summing him up. "I'm much obliged," he said as he offered a sweaty hand to Rodger.

"Thank you," said Rodger, shaking his hand. "But it wasn't me, it was my son AJ."

"And Bodo!" said AJ.

"Bodo? Who's Bodo?" asked the mayor.

"He's my dog, sir," said AJ, suddenly sad. The mayor didn't notice.

"Well, I'm sure mighty grateful to you both—and after this is all settled," he motioned toward the woods, "I'm sure we can arrange a reward for your help—Say, Dempsky, that reminds me, have you got that ten-thousand-dollar-police dog the city bought you guys out there searching for my aunt?"

Dempsky looked down at his shoes and replied, "Ah, no Sir, I'm afraid the dog and O'Conner are in Miami today getting re-certified."

"What! You mean to tell me we spent all that money for some high-fullutin' police dog and the first time I need it, it's off on some holiday!" shouted the stout little mayor, his belly jiggling with every syllable.

"I'm sorry, sir, but it's required by la—"

"Don't tell me the law! I *am* the law around here! Are you bringing in another dog? Pasco County's got one!" shouted the angry mayor.

"No Sir, we just got on the scene and there isn't enough time, sir, we couldn't get it here fast enou—"

"Bodo can do it!" shouted AJ.

Rodger, caught off guard, looked hard at his son, searching his eyes, then he turned to Officer Dempsky. "He's right, Bodo is a trained tracking dog. He can do it!"

"Well, where is he. Go get him! Dempsky, send a squad car!"

Dempsky screwed up his face to imply a problem.

"What's wrong now?" the mayor asked.

"Well, it's just that the dog is being confined for attacking the Bozwell kid. Clinton's got his lawyers on it. There's nothing we can do. Our hands are tied."

The mayor was not happy. He spoke very slowly and deliberately, punctuating each word with a stab in the air at Dempsky, "You mean to tell me, the mayor of this city, that we have a trained tracking dog sitting in our pound while my helpless, old aunt is wandering around in the woods during a forest fire? Get me the chief, now!"

The chief arrived quickly and explained to the mayor that he was duty-bound to uphold the law. He didn't have the authority to release the dog.

The mayor paced back and forth for a minute then bellowed, "Where's Clinton Bozwell?"

"He's in the second car," answered the Chief.

"Well, go get him!"

Clinton Bozwell had been sitting in the squad car talking angrily to his lawyer on his cell phone. He had not seen Rodger arrive. But he saw him now, as he was led to the mayor. He felt the rage boil up in his throat.

"What's he doing here?" Bozwell asked the chief who

led him by the arm toward the mayor.

"Bozwell," snapped the mayor, "I understand you've got a complaint against this man's dog,"

"Complaint! I've got a team of lawyers working on it right now," he said, turning to Rodger. "By the time I'm done with you, you'll never see that vicious dog of yours alive again!"

Rodger, outwardly calm, stood his ground and said nothing. But inside, the anger and loathing he felt for this greedy and devious man clawed at his insides.

"Dad, what's he gonna' do to Bodo, what did he mean?" asked AJ.

"Never mind, son, I'll handle this," said Rodger, his gaze locked on Clinton's, matching the ice-cold stare with his own.

The mayor intervened. "Now, Mr. Bozwell, you and I are men of business and as such we both know that in business, one hand washes the other."

Bozwell now eyed the mayor suspiciously. "Now, if I were to promise you that my son Charles would drop the charges against your son for stealing the watch, would you be inclined to drop the charges against the dog?"

Clinton thought a minute. "No deal!" he snapped.

AJ's heart fell. "So what if you drop the charges on one watch, he's facing a lot more than that. What difference would it make? You're going to have to do a lot better than that."

"Hmm," said the mayor, planning his next move. "I see your point. Well, Clinton, I am a man of, shall we say—considerable influence in this town, and here is what I propose. You will drop the charges against the dog and the family, in exchange for my promise that my office will do everything it can to guarantee your son will be tried as a juvenile. If convicted, he'll most likely do a very light sentence in Juvenile Hall and be home by Christmas, his record sealed. If you don't agree, I promise you I'll use every ounce of influence I possess as mayor to have that boy tried as an adult. Then he'll be facing the maximum sentence under the law. Now do we have a deal?"

The last question was asked with a chilling tone, an unexpected show from the outwardly genteel mayor.

Bozwell wanted to spit in the mayor's face. "It's a deal," he grumbled, the words sticking in his throat.

"Excellent," said the mayor. "We'll put it all in writing." He snapped his fingers and his chauffeur, who was also his clerk, jumped to attention, pen in hand. He turned to Dempsky, "Officer, order that dog Bo-bo. . ."

"Bodo," yelled Rodger and AJ.

"Sorry. *Bodo* brought here immediately!"

"I'll need his tracking gear!" said AJ,

"No problem!" said officer Dempsky, "Hop in." AJ held back a second looking over at Billy Bozwell who glared at him, but remembering the handcuffs, regained his courage and strutted over to the other side of the squad car and jumped in. They sped off at top speed.

Officer Dempsky grabbed the mic and ordered the dispatcher to have an officer bring Bodo to the nursing home immediately. He then reached over and flipped on the siren and flashing lights.

Rodger rejoined Hannah and told her what they were planning to try with Bodo.

"Do you know if he can do it?" she asked.

"Well I'm not one-hundred percent sure," said Rodger. "But at least ninety-nine."

AJ was having the thrill of his life. Speeding down the main boulevard through town at top speed, red lights flashing, siren wailing and Bodo on his way to him!

Suddenly his mood changed as he realized he actually didn't know where or how to begin. He knew how to tell Bodo to find gold, but how would he tell him to find a person? As thoughts of doubt swirled around in his head, he was beginning to tremble. He tried to recall what his teacher had told the class about tracking. Schutzhund 1 required the dog to follow a track at least twenty minutes old with two right-angle turns. Schutzhund 2 required a track at least thirty minutes old with two turns, but over a longer distance. Schutzhund 3, the most difficult challenge of all, required the dog to follow a track at least sixty minutes old, with at least four right-angle turns. *Sixty minutes*, he thought to himself and Miss Effie had already been missing almost that long.

He was suddenly filled with doubt. He realized it would take nothing less than an expert Schutzhund 3 level dog with years of training and practice to do this. He silently prayed Uncle Ivo had taught Bodo everything he needed to know.

Within minutes, the car pulled up at his house. He jumped out and ran as fast as he could to the garage to get his tracking gear. Becki and Nixie ran to the door expecting to see Rodger. When Becki saw the police car instead, she was terrified that something had happened to her parents. She grabbed Nixie's hand and ran out to the police car.

"What's happened?" she demanded. "Where is my father?"

The officer, with no time to explain and not sure what to tell the girls, said simply, "Get in, I'll take you to him, he's fine."

They climbed into the front seat as AJ ran back

carrying Bodo's gear.

Seeing the girls in the front, he had no choice but to climb into the back next to Bozwell. As they sped back to the nursing home, AJ told Becki about Miss Effie and that they were getting Bodo out of the pound to attempt a rescue.

Becki's eyes began to fill with tears at the thought of Miss Effie caught in a fire. "Oh, AJ, Bodo can do it, I know he can."

"That worthless mutt of yours couldn't find beef in a butcher shop if you ask me," mumbled Billy Bozwell.

"Well no one asked you," snapped Officer Dempsky. Nixie then turned around on the seat and stuck her tongue out at Bozwell. AJ didn't see it. He was too absorbed in trying to remember if he had learned anything yet about tracking people.

"It's not Bodo I'm worried about," AJ said out loud.

"What's the matter, Son?" asked Dempsky.

"Well, it's just that, I don't exactly know how to do this. I mean I know Bodo can find jewelry—"

Bozwell snorted.

"But I've never done this. What if I mess up? What if Miss Effie dies?" As he spoke he stared down at his trembling hands.

Officer Dempsky thought a few seconds then reached

for his car radio. "Dispatch, I want you to track down O'Conner in Miami and patch me through to his cell phone. I know he's in class, but we have a situation here."

Within seconds O'Conner was on the line. Officer Dempsky quickly brought him up to speed, and assured him that his wife Shelly, one of the nurses, was in no immediate danger. O'Conner then hung up and immediately called back on Dempsky's cell phone. The officer handed the cell phone to AJ just as they pulled into the nursing home. Bodo had not yet arrived.

Becki and Nixie jumped out of the car and ran to Hannah, who was glad to see them. AJ was getting much needed instructions from O'Conner. He climbed out of the squad car and went over to his mother, still holding the phone to one ear. A small crowd began to form around him that included the mayor, AJ's family, residents and nursing home staff.

Clinton Bozwell watched too, but from a distance.

"Yes, Sir, I understand," said AJ, turning to Hannah.

"Mom, I need something with Miss Effie's scent on it, preferably an upper-body-garment," he said, repeating the words carefully. Hannah thought for an instant, and then Terry Langley spoke up.

"Hannah! Her shawl, I brought it to her this morning but she didn't want it so I remember laying it over the back of her chair. I'll get it!" she said, turning to race to the sun porch where Miss Effie had been sitting.

"Don't touch it!" screamed AJ. Terry froze. AJ, with the phone still to his ear, turned to Hannah again.

"Mom—I need two things—fast!" he said. She immediately dropped Nixie's hand and waited for instructions. AJ stopped listening and said, "I need a coat hanger and a clean plastic bag with no smell on it, big enough to hold the shawl!"

Hannah raced into the nursing home through the parting crowd. All eyes were now fixed on the boy.

At that instant, the car bringing Bodo screeched to a halt behind Dempsky's car. Upon a signal from Dempsky the officer opened the back door to let Bodo out. Bodo bounded out and charged joyfully toward AJ, who opened his arms wide to hug his dog, but quickly recovered and went right to work.

He handed the phone to Officer Dempsky and grabbed the harness from the back of the car. He secured Bodo into it as fast as he could. Bodo knew the harness meant work and immediately became all business. Hannah ran through the crowd with the items. She had taken the extra precaution of throwing on a pair of rubber gloves to keep her scent off them.

Officer Dempsky now passed instructions to AJ. "Use

the coat hanger to pick up the shawl and drop it completely into the bag." The entire crowd now followed as AJ and Bodo ran around back to the sun porch following nurse Langley. He ran to the chair she pointed to and easily hooked the shawl with the coat hanger and dropped it into the plastic bag Hannah held open. "Now take Bodo to the *PLS* and—"

"The what?" asked AJ.

"The what?" said Dempsky into the phone. Then to AJ, he said, "Sorry, he means the point last seen."

AJ turned to Hannah again for help. She turned to Terry.

"Over here!" said Terry, leading the way. The crowd started to follow, until Officer Dempsky ordered everyone to stay back to keep the area from being tainted. Nurse Langley led AJ to the spot where Henry said Miss Effie had vanished.

"OK, AJ," said Dempsky, reciting verbatim the instructions he was getting from Sergeant O'Conner. "Now I want you to go to Bodo with the plastic bag, hold it open and let him sniff it very deeply for about ten seconds. Then I want you to give him the command, *Search*—no, wait . . . what? Such?"

AJ broke in, "It's German. Bodo was trained in German."

"Oh, yeah, I forgot," said Dempsky. "Are you ready?"

"We're ready." AJ opened the bag and held it for Bodo. As Bodo sniffed it, AJ whispered to him. "You gotta' do this boy, you've got to find her. If you do, I know they'll let you come home. You can do it, boy."

Then he stood up and handed the bag to Officer Dempsky, took a deep breath and said loud enough for all to hear, "Such!" Rodger held his breath, Hannah silently prayed to Uncle Ivo, Mayor Pennywell watched anxiously, and Bodo took off!

The search party ran toward the woods trying to keep up with Bodo, who had picked up the scent instantly. As they ran, Officer Dempsky kept feeding more information to AJ from O'Conner, "Now children and very old confused people don't walk in a straight line—they zigzag around—so don't worry if Bodo appears to go in circles—and use the plastic bag again if he stops for too long."

Bodo was pulling ahead at a very rapid pace and quickly entered the forest. Dempsky, Mayor Pennywell and two other officers followed them. They had difficulty keeping up. Bodo trotted first in one direction for several long minutes then did almost a complete about face, just as O'Conner had told him he might, then another direction change, then another. Minutes seemed like hours. He pulled them closer and closer into the direction of the fire.

The smoke was beginning to get frighteningly close. AJ was afraid that if the wind changed, the smoke would obscure the scent trail. On and on they went, deeper into the forest. Then Bodo did something odd. He froze for a few long seconds and lifted his head. He began to sniff the air, then he lopped off in a straight line, not the winding trail they had been following, his nose no longer to the ground. AJ had spent the entire summer tracking behind Bodo and knew that Bodo's nose never left the ground when he worked. Dempsky was reporting Bodo's every move to O'Conner. On the other end of the phone, O'Conner shouted, "He did what! Are you sure?"

"I'm positive!" said Dempsky, a little out of breath as they hurried to keep up. "I'm telling you he's going great guns with his nose up, and he's not winding around like before. We're running in a straight line. Should we stop him?"

"No! Let him go, but, man, that's impressive, Harry, he's *air scenting!* That means she's really close. It's just that—, well, a dog that trails is hardly ever trained to air scent! It's usually one or the other. Geez, Harry, that dog has been dual trained!"

Bodo pulled them deeper into the forest. Then he suddenly froze. AJ ran ahead to look. All he saw was a pile of twigs and debris. Bodo put his nose to the pile and nudged it several times. As AJ got closer, he saw her! He fell to his knees as the others caught up and surrounded him. Miss Effie lay there semi-conscious, at the foot of a small hill, which she must have tumbled down, judging by the twigs and forest debris covering her. Mayor Pennywell pushed his way to the front. Ignoring the officer's instructions to wait for an EMT, he gently lifted her frail body in his arms and carried her out of the forest himself.

Sergeant O'Conner had overseen the effort from a classroom in Miami filled with canine officers and their dogs. Everyone in the room had fallen silent to watch and listen as he guided the boy and his dog through the difficult rescue.

When he finally turned and yelled, "They got her!" a shouting roar went up. They were as thrilled as if they had actually been there themselves. Amid the loud cheers and congratulatory back slaps, O'Conner finally signed off and just stood there in a daze holding the dead phone.

He still couldn't believe what had just happened. *Man*, he thought to himself, shaking his head from side to side, a dog that can trail *and* air scent—*Geeeez*—that's a whole lot more dog than I imagined!

CHAPTER THIRTEEN

FRONT PAGE NEWS

Jumping up from the breakfast table in shock, Rodger knocked over his mug of coffee and stared wide-eyed at the front page of the morning paper.

"DOG AIDES MAYOR IN DARING RESCUE." The photo accompanying it had been taken at the exact moment Mayor Pennywell emerged from the woods. It showed him gently cradling the frail form of Miss Effie with Bodo beside him gazing up at them. AJ was just behind the two smiling. Rodger was not aware that a reporter was even present.

Yesterday had been a whirlwind of confusion. The crowd let out a cheer as nurses and doctors ran to meet the search party with a stretcher. There was no time for "thank-yous" and none were required. Rodger had gathered up his family and removed them from the chaos quickly to help clear the scene. AJ climbed into the van, then remembered the peanut butter jar and ran back to give it to Officer Dempsky. He was happy to be free of it. It had caused him nothing but trouble. He was thrilled to have Bodo back home and had spent the rest of the day pampering, praising and playing with him.

Rodger lay down the newspaper and grabbed some paper towels to mop up the spilled coffee, then poured another cup and sat back down to read the article just as the phone rang. It would not stop ringing for the next three days.

The article covering the rescue included a statement from the mayor praising both Bodo and AJ Jenkins for their heroism and effort. It went on to describe how Bodo had skillfully followed a winding trail in spite of the advancing fire to locate the obscured and semi-conscious Miss Effie after search parties had been scouring the area unsuccessfully for almost an hour. But that was not the reason the phone was ringing. Just below that article was another headline that read, **"DOG FINDS GOLD!"**

The first call had been long distance, very long distance from a man offering to buy Bodo, for two million yen. Rodger, flabbergasted, had gotten rid of him abruptly, hanging up just to have it ring again and again. By this time the ringing phone was waking up the entire house. As Rodger dealt with yet another call, Hannah shuffled out to the kitchen in her robe, and he handed her the paper, front page up. As he wrapped up the call, she heard him tell the person that Bodo could not possibly find a ring that went down the drain two years ago. She then stared down at the newspaper, shocked. Rodger hung up and it immediately rang again.

He asked the caller to hold and turned to Hannah, "Hon, you're not gonna' believe this—people have actually been calling with offers to buy Bodo—or to hire him to search for lost jewelry."

Hannah shook her head disapprovingly and took her coffee and the newspaper to the living room. The article about Bodo finding gold included a lost and found phone number for people to call and identify their lost items from AJ's peanut butter jar. AJ had decided to donate any unclaimed jewelry to his friend Crabby Gus anonymously. Hannah was glad to think that AJ's efforts would end up doing some good, but she didn't care one bit for these strange calls.

The calls continued throughout the day. Rodger sat by the phone and dealt with every request. He patiently explained to hopeful callers about the suntan lotion and apologized that he could not help them, with two exceptions. Two of the callers had been at the beach very recently, were wearing sunscreen or lotion and had lost something valuable.

Rodger, though reluctant, eventually gave in. AJ was

glad to attempt a search. They arranged to meet both callers at the beach after dinner.

As they sat down to dinner, once again, the phone rang. "I'll get this one," said Hannah.

"Hello?—Yes—Oh, hello!—Really—Why, that would be wonderful!—Of course—Yes—Thank you so much!" Then turning to her family beaming, "You won't believe this. That was the mayor's office. They want to give AJ and Bodo an award!"

"An award!" said AJ grinning. "Wow, Bodo did you hear that!"

"Way to go!" said Rodger.

"They're planning to present it at the Founder's Day celebration! I am so proud of you guys," she said tousling AJ's hair. "You're my heroes!"

"Oh, AJ, I knew Bodo could do it!" beamed Becki. "My little brother, a town hero!"

After the family finished their meal, smiling and laughing at the excitement of the day, Rodger, AJ and Bodo set off to meet the two callers at the beach. The first meeting place was the parking lot at Sea Otter Cove. AJ strapped Bodo into his harness while a kindly middle-aged woman explained how she had lost her mother's ring. The ring was 14kt. gold with six birthstones set in it, one stone for each of her six children. She believes she lost it after putting sunscreen on her grandchildren, then wiping her hands clean on a rough towel. She had owned the ring for more than twenty years. AJ was very anxious to help, seeing how upset the woman was.

"Can you remember where you were sitting?" he asked, ready to begin.

"Oh my, yes. We were right over here by the rest rooms," she said, leading the way. "Yes, right about here."

AJ and Bodo started the search. "Find the Gold!" AJ commanded, and Bodo went right to work. He started at the spot where the woman had pointed and began weaving back and forth. Bodo searched for less then four minutes before laying down about ten feet from where they started.

AJ ran over and scooped through the sand, pulling up the ring triumphantly! Rodger stood watching, dumbstruck. By now he had of course heard how Bodo found gold, but actually seeing it was another story. The woman cried tears of joy. She had been certain she would never see her ring again. She ran back to her car and grabbed her purse pulling out a fifty dollar bill. AJ refused as convincingly as he could, but she would not allow them to leave without the reward. He eventually accepted with much chagrin, and they said goodbye.

Next, they headed to the second meeting place,

Moccasin Head Point. There they were to meet a man who was desperately trying to locate his girlfriend's missing gold bracelet. They pulled into the parking lot and looked around. The lot was empty but they were very early. The first search had gone much quicker than expected. With time to kill, they got out and walked around, ending up at the path to the Point, and proceeded down it. After showing his father where Bodo had found the watch, they headed back to the parking lot to see if the man had arrived. As they approached the lot, they saw a dirty black SUV pull in next to their van. Two men got out. Rodger was immediately on guard.

One man was short and very stocky, with long stringy dark hair. The other man was tall and scrappy-looking, unshaven with dirty, blonde hair hanging in his eyes. He wore several gold chains around his neck and a dirty gray muscle shirt. Rodger would have liked to avoid the meeting altogether but it was too late. He made his way to where they stood leaning on their beat up SUV. They introduced themselves as Murry and Floyd. Rodger had a strong suspicion they were up to no good. AJ, oblivious to his father's apprehension spoke up. "What will we be searching for?" he asked.

The skinny man spoke, "Well, my girlfriend, she lost her favorite necklace on the beach the other day an' then

I saw this here article about some dog that finds gold—
and I sez to Murry, I sez—I wonder if that there dog can
find that necklace."

"I thought you said bracelet on the phone?" asked
Rodger, now convinced he wanted nothing to do with
these two characters. The skinny man chatted on and on.
As Rodger stood there sizing them up, he glanced through
the mud-covered window into the back of the SUV. What
he saw sent chills up his spine.

"Oh yeah, necklace, bracelet—somethin' gold is allz I
know for sure. So how's this work? You just set him loose
and he digs up gold?"

"Well, not exactly," said Rodger, attempting to keep
his voice level, "Actually, that article wasn't really true."

AJ snapped his head around to look at his father,
confused. "What do you mean, Dad?" he asked. "Bodo
finds gol—." Rodger cut him off and shot him a look.

"Now, Son, you know what I told you. You have to
come clean and tell these men the truth."

"But Dad—"

"The truth, son, now tell them how you were using
a metal detector all along to find all that stuff. Go on,
tell them."

AJ knew something was very wrong. He could see the
warning in his father's eyes. His heart began to race and

his instincts told him to play along, though he didn't know why, but he trusted his father.

"Yes, it's true. I was lying. I'm real sorry I dragged you all the way out here," he said.

"I told you!" said the stocky man, "I knew it was a lie. You and your dumb ideas. A dog that can smell gold. Yeah right. How stupid do you gotta' be to swallow that one? I'm out'a' here."

He turned and got in his vehicle and slammed the door. His friend eyed Rodger suspiciously then turned and left. Rodger told AJ to get in the van. They waited until the SUV disappeared before AJ spoke. "What happened Dad? Why didn't we help them?"

"I'm sorry about that, Son, I just had a really bad feeling about those guys. I think they were up to no good. Actually," he continued after a long pause, "I think Bodo's prospecting days may be over."

They rode home in silence, AJ deep in thought. He slowly began to realize that there could be people in this world who would do anything to get their hands on a dog that could find gold. A dog like Bodo. It's something he never would have thought of, until tonight. As they pulled up to the house, he turned to his father and said, "I think you're right Dad. Bodo's prospecting days are definitely over."

AJ would never know what his father had seen in the back of that black SUV. It was a brand new stainless steel dog crate with the price tag still on it—and it was large enough to hold Bodo.

CHAPTER FOURTEEN

THE ANNOUNCEMENT

Founder's day in the little town of Gulfside Beach was a very big event. Unlike the Fourth of July, which draws many visitors and tourists, this celebration was for the townsfolk. It was traditionally a time when everyone turned out for the day-long potluck picnics, to meet the newcomers and to renew old acquaintances. The festivities would begin at noon on the town green and go throughout the evening with a disc jockey for the young and a twelve-piece swing-band for the young at heart.

Two of the three large gazebos would host a different type of entertainment. A popular touring puppet show would be performing in one for the local children, and the town's State Champion marching band in the other.

The third gazebo had been decked out in bright, multi-colored crepe paper and banners and was the location where Mayor Pennywell would conduct the opening ceremonies, and update the townsfolk on any new or old business.

This year the shipyard was the subject that had the town abuzz. The rumors reached Rodger last evening. He was in the garage working on his van when Benny raced over to tell him what he heard. "It's all over town, Rog, that's what they're saying. It's almost a done deal! My cousin, Midge, who works in the cubical next to Brenda Hathaway, heard her talking to her son, who works in the title company—"

"As an apprentice clerk, Benny," said Rodger.

"Yeah, but he says it's been sold, Rog. What do you make of it?"

Rodger put down the spark plug wrench and wiped his hands on a towel while he thought it through.

"Boy, Rog, wouldn't that be something?"

"If it's true," said Rodger. "I think I'd wait until you're absolutely sure before celebrating, Ben. I mean, even if it is true, who's to say the new owner is going to want us back, or for that matter, who's to say they're not going to knock it down and throw up a bunch of those new waterfront condos?"

Benny, having not considered that possibility, looked wide eyed at Rodger, his thick brows knotted. "Geeeez, Rog, I hadn't thought of that. You don't think that's possible, do you?"

"I don't know, Benny, that's just the point. Nobody

knows anything for sure."

"Yeah, I guess you're right. Well, I gotta' go make some calls," he mumbled as he turned to go.

He's right about one thing, thought Rodger. The rumor is all over town. Everyone was talking. With so many families affected by the shipyard closing, savings were dwindling and fear was running rampant. It's no wonder they were latching on to the tiniest glimmer of hope. He finished cleaning his tools, returned them to their places and went inside for dinner.

"How's the van?" asked Hannah.

"Oh, I think it'll hold up for another hundred thousand miles," he said, as he washed up at the sink.

"Say, did Benny have any more news?" she asked.

"Now, Hannah, you know better than to put much stock in anything Benny says."

"Oh, don't be so hard on him," she said. "He's just as worried as the rest of us. Let's just hope that at least one rumor turns out to be true."

"Which one?" he asked.

"The one about the mayor making some big announcement tomorrow."

"Becki, what's taking you so long!" shouted AJ, "I don't want to be late! Everyone's in the van. Come on!"

"I just need to find something! I've got it now," she said running out the door past him to jump into the van, waving Bodo's red bandanna in the air. "He has to look good for his award. The whole town will be there!"

AJ rolled his eyes and pulled the door closed.

At the mention of the award, he felt a wave of butterflies descend on his stomach. He was more than a little nervous about climbing up onto the stage with the entire town watching. The mayor's office had phoned yesterday to confirm AJ and Bodo's appearance at noon.

Hannah was as excited as AJ. "It's not everyday my son gets an award for being a hero!" she said, much to AJ's embarrassment. "Rodger, did you remember the camera?"

"For the third time, Hannah, yes. Now let's go or we'll miss the whole thing."

"Daddy," said Nixie, "Am I really going to see Pinky the Goose at the puppet show?"

"Absolutely," said Rodger. "And all of his friends too!"

"Yeah!" she squealed, clapping her hands.

Rodger found a parking space and the family headed over to the pavilion where the mayor's coordinator was waiting for them. She sat them in the front row and told them everything was almost under way so not to wander off.

The band began to play and soon they found themselves at the front of a sea of anxious faces. Everyone in town had turned out. Hundreds of people packed onto the grass around the many rows of folding chairs.

There was standing room only as far as AJ could see. Soon the mayor's limo was spotted making its way to the back of the pavilion. The crowd cheered as the mayor got out and waved, then turned back to the limo to help Miss Effie out and into an awaiting wheelchair.

Upon seeing the beloved old teacher appear on the stage, the crowd cheered loudly. Everyone in town knew and adored Miss Effie. Next old Henry Jones appeared from inside the limo smiling broadly as he was helped onto the stage in his wheelchair.

Another limo pulled up and more people got out. AJ recognized Sergeant O'Conner as he took a seat on the stage.

Taking a seat beside him, AJ was surprised to see Konrad Hartmann, his Schutzhund instructor. He wasn't sure why he was up there, but the thought of his presence calmed AJ. He was very proud Mr. Hartmann would know how well Bodo had done.

The mayor, in a starched white suit and as usual, sweating profusely, finally approached the microphone. After thanking everyone for being there, Mayor

Pennywell got right down to business. AJ's stomach was doing flips.

"Citizens of Gulfside Beach, it is my distinguished pleasure today to honor a young man to whom I am personally indebted and especially grateful. This brave young man, along with his remarkable dog, single-handedly led a rescue party into a burning forest to save the life of someone very near and dear to many of us."

He turned and smiled at Miss Effie, who raised her frail hand up in a tiny triumphant fist. The crowd clapped and cheered.

"It is with great pleasure that I ask young Alec Jenkins and his dog Bodo to please come up."

The crowd clapped as AJ, weak in the knees, gathered his courage along with Bodo's leash and proudly climbed the steps and stood beside the mayor.

"And now to present the award, I would like to introduce our own canine expert, Sergeant Mike O'Conner." The crowd clapped as Sergeant O'Conner approached the microphone.

"Thank you, Mr. Mayor, this is a great honor for me to be here today. And on behalf of the Gulfside Beach Police Department and the city of Gulfside Beach, we would like to present to Alec Jenkins this very special award of heroism and gratitude."

He then handed AJ a mounted gold plaque that read, "To Alec Joseph Jenkins and his canine partner Bodo, in appreciation of their acts of bravery in a time of crisis, from a grateful community."

O'Conner then reached into his pocket and took out a small wooden box. He opened the lid and pulled out a red ribbon with a large gold medallion attached to it. It read, "Honorary Deputy, Gulfside Beach Brotherhood of Police," and slipped it over AJ's head.

AJ was bursting with pride. "And now, to present a very special award to Bodo, I would like to introduce the foremost authority on police dog training in the state of Florida, Mr. Konrad Hartmann."

AJ grinned from ear to ear at his Schutzhund instructor. Now he understood. Bodo was getting an award too.

"Thank you, Sergeant O'Conner," began Hartmann, "Ladies and Gentlemen—I am a *Schutzhund* trainer."

"A what?" murmured the crowd. "What did he say? A shootzum, what?"

"A Schutzhund trainer. Now I know most of you here today have never heard that word before. Please allow me to explain. In Germany, where I come from, Schutzhund is both a sport and a very intense training program for working dogs.

249

Bodo has been my student for three months now, but I am here to tell you today that I have taught him nothing!" He paused here for this to sink in, as he looked across the puzzled faces in the crowd.

"This does not mean he was not trained. Bodo Von Bremik was bred and trained in Germany by one of Europe's best-known experts in the sport of Schutzhund, long before ever setting foot—I mean *paw*—on American soil. Sadly, this dedicated man did not live to see the fruits of his labor. His name was Ivo Bremik. A name so well known in the world of boxers and Schutzhund, that it reaches us all the way over here in America. This remarkable dog, Bodo Von Bremik, represents the accomplishments of a lifetime of hard work, meticulous breeding and expert training in an unending effort to strive for perfection in the breed of boxers and in the sport of Schutzhund. And though, sadly, Ivo Bremik never had the opportunity to trial Bodo, he most certainly trained him. I have seen many wonderful and highly skilled dogs graduate from my training course after years of effort and hard work, but this is the first time I have ever had one enter that way."

The crowd laughed and clapped and Hannah's heart swelled with emotion as she listened to the man honor Uncle Ivo.

"There are three specific skills in which a Schutzhund dog must excel in order to be awarded a title, and there are three levels of title, Schutzhund 1, 2 and 3. Each level requires the dog to be proficient in all three skills. As you progress higher in level, the skills become much more difficult. The first is tracking. A Schutzhund Dog must be able to track, and I think we all now know that when it comes to tracking, that dog can hunt!"

A cheer went up and the crowd laughed at the pun. Miss Effie raised her fist again in triumph. "The second is obedience, and I have seen first-hand Bodo's loyal and obedient nature. A Schutzhund dog must be able to do many things on command, such as retrieve dumbbells . . ."

"You mean like *Bozzy*?" shouted someone from the crowd. Everyone laughed heartily at this, all having heard the story by now.

"Um—well—and the last skill is protection. A Schutzhund dog must know how to protect its master and how to detain an aggressor until ordered to release. In the—uh—recent apprehension of an alleged burglar."

"You mean the *dumbbell*?" shouted another man grinning at his own wit, amid roars of laughter from the crowd.

"Bodo demonstrated an expert level of knowledge and skill in the area of protection. And so, based on my three decades of experience as a Schutzhund trainer and certified judge, it is within my authority to grant to this exceptional dog—the title of Schutzhund 3—the highest level of accomplishment for a Schutzhund dog!"

The roar of the crowd was tremendous. People jumped from their seats and whooped and hollered happily as Hartmann handed AJ the official framed certificate. He then placed around Bodo's neck a gold medal, the same as AJ's. Bodo stood obediently, smiling at the crowd, enjoying the attention. AJ was bursting with pride. Finally descending the stage amid more cheers and clapping, he thought himself the luckiest kid in the world. AJ took his seat and after waiting for the crowd to settle, Mayor Pennywell took the stage again.

"And now, citizens of Gulfside Beach, on to another matter that I know is on the minds of everyone. I know many of you have been hearing rumors around town concerning the fate of our own shipyard. And I know how difficult it has been these past few months for many of you and your families. I am here today to officially announce that after much negotiation and hard work by members of my dedicated staff and many other people as well, Bravetti Marine has a new owner and will soon open it's doors again!"

The crowd went wild, cheering, clapping and crying

tears of relief and joy. "And now, it gives me great pleasure to introduce you to Gulfside Beach's newest benefactor." He turned all attention to the limo behind him, as a man stepped out. With great poise, he climbed up onto the podium. An attractive middle-aged woman followed the man out of the limo. Next came three younger women, all very stylishly attired. The last to emerge had in her hands a leash. As she was busy trying to coax a reluctant animal out of the limo, Rodger and Hannah gasped as they stared up at the familiar face. "... *Captain Viktor Wilhelm Adler!*" continued the mayor.

The cheers were deafening. The crowd was jubilant. There was hugging and hand-shaking, pounding of feet and thumping of backs! This was the answer to their prayers and the town made their gratitude known to the welcome stranger.

After several long moments of cheering, Viktor smiled graciously and nodded to the crowd as he stepped up to the microphone. "It is not often," he began with a smile, "zat I vould take second place to a dog, but because it is Herr Bodo, it is as it should be. You see, ve are old friends! Bodo my friend, *Komm!*"

AJ unhooked his leash as Bodo rose quickly to obey, hopped up onto the stage and hurried to Viktor's side. Viktor reached down to pet his friend. Bodo's tail spun in circles with joy. "You see, Ladies und Gentleman, Herr Bodo vas ze first citizen of zis vonderful town zat I met. Und through him I vas to meet many new friends—und zis is how I am to be standing here today. So it is Herr Bodo zat ve need to thank for bringing us all together!"

The exuberant crowd burst into more cheers and someone began to chant—"*Bodo! Bodo! Bodo!*" as all joined in.

Viktor, clearly enjoying himself, smiled and waited for the crowd to settle before continuing. "Und now, if I may, I vish to introduce my family. My lovely vife Rosa, und my three beautiful daughters Greta, Birgit und Stef . . .vere is Steffe?"

"Here, Papa," came a young girl's voice from the direction of the limo. "She vill not budge, Papa!"

Viktor then shouted in the direction of the limo, "Tinka *Komm!*" Instantly the reluctant dog appeared, hopped onto the stage in a single graceful movement and wedged her way jealously between Bodo and her master. Bodo looked over at her and tilted his head. The crowd roared with delight at the sight. The Jenkins family stared up wide-eyed, for their second look ever at a purebred, champion German boxer in all its glory. She was magnificent. Just slightly smaller and lighter than Bodo, with a beautifully rich brindle coat, the same unmistakable muscular frame and well-defined structure he possessed, and, of course, the natural ears and long, expressive tail. She nuzzled Viktor for attention, and he was, for a few seconds, helplessly under her spell. He soon regained his composure and returned to the business at hand.

"Und now ze moment you have been vaiting for. It gives me great joy to announce ze grand opening of ze *Adler-Bravetti Marine!*" Again the crowd went wild! "Und I vas vondering . . . does anyvone know vere I can find ze people to build ze boats?" Laughter spread through the audience. Viktor caught Hannah's eye in the crowd and winked. Hannah, now wondering what he was up to, smiled back curiously. He continued, "Und anyvone vishing to find vork is velcome to contact my new plant supervisor, Mr. Rodger Jenkins." Rodger, afraid he may have heard it wrong, shot a questioning glance at Viktor. Viktor smiled over at him and gave him a slight nod of assurance that it was real.

Hannah was beyond surprised, she was crying. Tears ran down her face as she silently sent out a prayer of thanks to her Uncle Ivo, a man who's entire legacy existed in a few cardboard boxes and a dog.

But what a dog, she thought as she looked up lovingly at Bodo. He was standing on the stage gently nudging the female on her ear. It seemed to her a lifetime ago that she received that call from Germany asking if they wanted the dog. She chuckled now at the question, and at how, back then, she didn't quite know what to imagine Bodo would be like.

"*Do we want the dog?*"

The question now seemed absurd. Bodo had pranced his way into their lives and into their hearts, bringing with him all that Ivo Bremik had to give.

And because of that gift, their lives and the fate of an entire town had been changed forever. Hannah's heart overflowed with gratitude to the uncle she had never met and to the dog he had loved. The man was gone now, but his legacy lived on in the heart of this one amazing dog. A dog that was so much more than she could have *ever* imagined.